Lightning flashed on the horizon.

"Well, I suggest you get a move on, then, because the clock is ticking. Surely I don't need to remind you that if you fail and the crowds don't come, the rodeo will be no more."

Thunder rumbled as he turned to glare at her. "No, I don't need to be reminded."

"Good." She pushed to her feet and moved his way until they were toe-to-toe. "Because I saw Kyleigh practice. She's passionate about what she's doing and is giving it her all. So I'd hate to think you're willing to let her down by settling for a so-so promotion campaign that will lead to the demise of the Hope Crossing Fair and Rodeo."

Let her down? Those three little words felt like a verbal punch in the gut. He'd let his wife down when she'd needed him most. And he never wanted to feel that way again.

He stared at the woman in front of him, despising the inclination that she seemed to be their only hope for saving the rodeo. Agreeing to work with Gloriana was risky, at best.

Award-winning author **Mindy Obenhaus** lives on a ranch in Texas with her husband, two sassy pups, and countless cattle and deer. She's passionate about touching readers with biblical truths in an entertaining, and sometimes adventurous, manner. When she's not writing, you'll usually find her in the kitchen, spending time with family or roaming the ranch. She'd love to connect with you via her website, mindyobenhaus.com.

Visit the Author Profile page at LoveInspired.com.

The Cowgirl's Redemption

Mindy Obenhaus

LOVE INSPIRED

INSPIRATIONAL ROMANCE

LOVE INSPIRED®
INSPIRATIONAL ROMANCE

Recycling programs
for this product may
not exist in your area.

ISBN-13: 978-1-335-58521-9

The Cowgirl's Redemption

Copyright © 2022 by Melinda Obenhaus

For questions and comments about the quality of this book, please contact us at CustomerService@Harlequin.com.

Love Inspired
22 Adelaide St. West, 41st Floor
Toronto, Ontario M5H 4E3, Canada
www.LoveInspired.com

Printed in U.S.A.

Therefore if any man be in Christ,
he is a new creature: old things are passed away;
behold, all things are become new.
—*2 Corinthians* 5:17

For Your Glory, Lord.

Acknowledgments

This book would not be what it is without the
help and input from many wonderful people
I am blessed to call friends. To Pamela Potter
and Gayle Coble, two of the most inspiring women
I've ever had the pleasure to know, God bless you.
To Terri Brasher, Amber McCarthy,
Cheryl Leyendecker and Becky Yauger,
thank you for helping me keep my facts straight.
I couldn't have done this without you. Hugs.

Chapter One

Gloriana Prescott had made a lot of mistakes in her life, and there were dozens of wrongs she needed to make right, but she wouldn't let her mother battle cancer alone.

Maneuvering her Jeep Cherokee off the county road where bluebonnets and Indian paintbrush danced across rolling hills, she passed under the arched metal Prescott Farms sign Saturday morning to continue up the long gravel drive lined with crepe myrtle trees that would boast bright pink blooms come summer. She scanned the pastures, silently thanking God for bringing her home safely. Something she'd never done before. Because until a few months ago, God wouldn't have even crossed her mind. Now, she trusted Him to guide her every step. Even when it meant giving up the job she'd worked so hard to achieve.

She rounded the final curve, her heart stopping as the flashing lights of an ambulance marred her first glimpse of the sprawling ranch house.

Pulse racing, she accelerated, glancing in her rearview mirror to see dust flying as a Chevy Silverado bore down

on her. Evidently, someone else was as desperate to get
to the house as she was.

God, please don't take Mom away from me now.

Gloriana had so much wasted time to make up for. She
wanted her mother to know that she'd changed. That she
wasn't merely offering lip service but had given her life
to Jesus and was trying hard to live in a manner that re-
flected that. Now she might never get that chance.

Gravel ground beneath her tires when she came to a
stop behind the ambulance parked in the circular drive.
She emerged from her vehicle into the surprisingly warm
morning air as someone slammed the door of the white
pickup behind her. A nanosecond later, the cowboy who'd
been driving jogged past her.

"What's happening?" She eyed the unfamiliar man.

"Don't know exactly," he tossed over his shoulder,
"but Mrs. Prescott isn't taking any visitors right now."

Visitor?

Ignoring his remark, she stepped onto the sidewalk
that led to the white-painted brick house, her steps halt-
ing as a girl met him on the covered front porch.

"I didn't know what to do." The child, who looked to
be in her early teens, sobbed as the man rubbed her arms.
"She was so pale. And she wouldn't wake up."

Gloriana froze, pressing a hand to her mouth as emo-
tion threatened to get the best of her. She was too late.
Mom was gone, and Gloriana had never gotten to say
goodbye. Just like Daddy.

"Calm down, sweetheart," the man said. "Let's see
what the EMTs have to say." His last statement jerked
Gloriana from her thoughts and gave her hope.

Emerging from the shade of the live oak that stood

sentry over the drive, she shielded her eyes from the sun until she reached the porch. "Excuse me."

Moving his hands to his Wrangler-clad hips, the man sporting a dark green T-shirt and a well-worn straw cowboy hat turned his pale blue-green eyes her way. "I'm sorry, miss. We have a bit of a crisis here. I don't think—"

She squared her shoulders. "My name is Gloriana Prescott. I'm Francine Prescott's daughter. So if there's something wrong with my mother, I suggest you get out of my way."

Looking from her to the girl and back, mouth agape, he said, "You're—"

"I don't have time for this." Gloriana moved around the teen, only to have him grab hold of her elbow before she reached the threshold. If looks could kill, he'd have fallen over from the intensity of her glare.

His gaze narrowed as he slowly released her. "How can I be sure you are who you say you are?"

The girl's dark brown eyes were wide as she wiped her tears. "That's Gloriana, Dad. I've seen her pictures."

Gloriana faced the adolescent, who was only a few inches shorter than her five foot six. Her chestnut-colored hair was in a ponytail that reached the middle of her back, and she had a smattering of freckles across her nose and cheeks. "What happened?" She willed her voice to remain calm. "To my mom."

"We were baking cookies, and she got real pale. Then she collapsed." The girl's voice cracked as fresh tears spilled onto her cheeks. "I called 9-1-1."

Unable to stop herself, Gloriana reached for the child's hand and gave it a squeeze. "You did just fine, sweetie." She released her as an EMT stepped out of the house.

"How is she?" the three asked in unison.

"She'll be fine." The man with a stethoscope draped around the neck of his dark blue shirt did a double take when he spotted Gloriana. "Well, I'll be." His slow grin hinted at an abundance of mischief-filled memories. "If it ain't Gloriana Prescott." Eric Chandler, a former classmate, wasted no time wrapping her in his beefy arms. "How you doin', girl?"

"I'd be better if I knew what was happening with my mother."

Releasing her, he took a step back to include the other man and his daughter.

"She just had a case of low blood sugar," said Eric. "You know, there's a reason they say breakfast is the most important meal of the day."

"But she was making cookies." Gloriana looked at the girl. "Did you see her eat anything? Maybe sample the dough?"

"No." She shook her head, her ponytail swaying. "She kept getting interrupted. People calling, texting, wanting to know about her surg—"

"You think it's really that simple?" Her father cut her off, his focus on Eric.

"Yes, sir. Brenda's got her sipping some orange juice and was trying to get her to eat a cookie when I came out here." Again, Eric's gaze shifted to Gloriana. "She said she skipped supper last night because she was feeling queasy and had only sipped black coffee today."

"Seriously?" Gloriana huffed out a breath. "Doesn't she know she should take better care of herself? Especially now. How does she expect to bounce back from surgery to battle cancer if she's not in the best health possible?"

The cowboy's eyebrows shot up. "You know about the cancer?"

While she had no idea who this guy was, it seemed he knew more about her mother than she did. And if Tori, her best friend since elementary school, hadn't called to say she was praying for Gloriana's mother, Gloriana would still be in the dark. Seemed Mom had no problem letting the entire church know about her upcoming surgery, yet she'd never said a word to Gloriana or her brother, Hawkins.

"You'll have to excuse me." She pushed her way into the house, continuing through the family room with its vaulted ceiling, wood floors and leather furniture before making a right into the country-style kitchen, where the sweet aroma of cookies still hung in the air. Her mother sat at the rustic wood table near the window, her blond bob slightly mussed, an EMT beside her.

"Gloriana?" Mom's dark eyes widened. "What—"

"I'm here to take care of you. And it appears I'm just in time. What are you trying to do, kill yourself?" Her words were harsh, but she couldn't help it.

"Whoa, now." The unknown cowboy stepped in front of her.

Looking around him to her mother, Gloriana said, "Who is this guy?"

"Oh, I guess you haven't met." Her mother gestured to the man and his daughter. "This is Justin Broussard, Prescott Farms ranch manager, and his daughter, Kyleigh."

"Hi." The girl waved shyly from beside her father.

Gloriana cringed. Why hadn't she figured that out on her own? She'd certainly heard plenty about Justin and Kyleigh over the past few years.

"Okay, Mrs. Prescott." The female EMT removed the blood pressure cuff. "Your vitals are much better. How are you feeling?"

Mom looked Gloriana's way. "A little stunned at the moment, but overall—"

"I got here as fast as I could." A tall cowboy whisked past Gloriana, making a beeline for her mother. Removing his hat, he knelt next to the woman. Only then did Gloriana recognize him. But why would Bill Krenek be so concerned about her mother?

"What happened, Francie?" He took hold of Mom's hand, though the woman promptly freed herself. Still, it seemed Bill's appearance had helped her mother, because her color was returning in short order, her cheeks suddenly a brilliant pink.

Gloriana looked at the older, rather handsome rancher who'd been a friend of her father's. The two used to help each other whenever it came time to work cattle, and Bill and his wife, Angie, and their daughter, Alli, would join them for cookouts and the annual Good Friday fish fry Gloriana's father used to put on. But why was Bill here now?

"Bill, you remember my daughter, Gloriana." Mom motioned in her direction as he stood, his cheeks now a shade similar to her mother's.

He nodded. "'Course I remember. Best barrel racer ever to come out of Hope Crossing." Hat now in one hand, he moved toward her and extended the other. "Good to have you back."

Taking hold of his callused fingers, she cocked her head, noting the gray creeping into his once light brown hair. "What brings you by?"

"Me?" Releasing her, he seemed to defer to her mother. "Oh, I, uh—"

"I promised him some spinach from my garden," her mother injected. "I've had quite the crop this year."

"And you hurried over here for that?" Gloriana's confused gaze moved from her mother to Bill. They wore the same guilty expression, as though they'd been caught—

Gloriana's eyes widened as a sudden wave of nausea had her winding her arms around her middle. Bill wasn't here because of her mother's garden; he was here because of the woman herself.

Her mother had a boyfriend!

In the buffet line of life, Justin Broussard's plate was not only piled high, but overflowing. Between single parenting, running Prescott Farms, preparing Ky for her first rodeo and foolishly volunteering to handle the advertising for Hope Crossing's annual fair and rodeo, he didn't have time to contend with Francie's prodigal daughter. The one he'd never laid eyes on during all of his three years at Prescott Farms but had heard plenty about.

Like how she'd had a bit of a wild streak as a teenager and skedaddled out of Hope Crossing right after graduation and never looked back. Not to mention how she was so preoccupied with her own life she hadn't even bothered to come home for her daddy's funeral.

Justin looked across the kitchen to the older Prescott woman still sitting at the table. The one who'd become like a second mother to him and a third grandmother to Ky. From the moment he and his daughter arrived at Prescott Farms, Francie had gone out of her way to make them feel at home. Not only did they live in a cabin on the property, but Francie had given them full access to the ranch, allowing them to keep their horses here and giving his daughter a place to practice her barrel racing. Throw in all the time she spent with Ky, teaching her to bake, garden and can, the countless meals she'd either invited them to share with her or delivered to their place, and, well, he'd become pretty protective of Francie.

So if Gloriana thought she could sweep in here with her perfectly styled hair, manicured nails and designer jeans in an effort to ease her conscience by acknowledging her mother existed, she'd better be prepared to deal with him.

"Um—" Seemingly trying to compose herself, Gloriana swiped her long, deep brown hair behind her ears, her hazel eyes darting around the room. "Would you all give me a moment alone with my mother, please?"

The EMTs were already packing up their gear while Bill and Justin exchanged wary looks. Neither was willing to throw Francie to the wolves. Even if said wolf was her only daughter.

"It's okay, fellas." Francie addressed the two men. "Glory and I have a lot to catch up on."

Not the least of which was her upcoming surgery. How had Gloriana found out about Francie's cancer? Not that Justin hadn't encouraged the woman to share the news with her children. To which she usually responded, "I don't want to bother them."

Justin shook his head. He knew for a fact her son, Hawkins, would want to know. He'd been home a handful of times since Justin had been here, and he lived all the way up in Alaska. Meanwhile, Gloriana was only two states away and he hadn't seen hide nor hair of her until now.

"Come on, Ky." He urged his daughter to follow the

EMTs toward the front of the house while Bill trailed behind.

Once on the porch, Bill looked at Justin, his expression grim. A slight shake of his head silently echoed Justin's displeasure of the sudden turn of events. Then he followed the EMTs to the ambulance, pausing to speak with them.

"Can you believe it, Dad?" Ky paused beside one of the four rocking chairs lining the porch.

He couldn't miss the spark in his fourteen-year-old daughter's dark eyes. "Believe what?"

"Mrs. Francie's daughter, *the barrel racer*, is here!"

"That was a long time ago." He eased into the wooden rocker beside her. "Back when she was your age."

"She's not *that* old." Ky dropped into the chair beside him.

He removed his hat long enough to drag a hand through his hair, desperate to deter his daughter. "Are you insinuating your old man is actually old?"

She laughed, a sound he'd never grow tired of hearing. "Well, you are forty."

"Barely." Frustration had him setting the rocker into motion. "She's a news reporter, Ky. She probably hasn't been in a saddle, let alone raced, for a very long time." And that was fine by him. He wasn't too keen on his daughter getting all starry-eyed over Gloriana Prescott.

"Maybe she could watch me practice," Ky continued. "She might be able to give me some pointers."

He admired his daughter's dedication to her sport. Yet while he'd do just about anything to help her win, he didn't want Ky spending even the smallest amount of time with Francie's daughter.

"Have you forgotten you already have a coach?"

"No." Ky picked at the frayed hole in her jeans. "But Mrs. Patty is kinda old."

"She still races, though."

"I know. But you heard Mr. Krenek." Excitement flickered in her eyes as she looked his way. "Mrs. Francie's daughter was one of *the best* barrel racers ever."

"In Hope Crossing." The town was barely a map dot. Something that suited Justin just fine. After seventeen years in the Dallas–Fort Worth metromess, he'd been more than ready to escape and get back to his roots. He might not have his own spread, but having grown up the son of a ranch manager, ranching was still in his blood. Too bad it had taken his wife's death to spur the move. But with Barbie's type one diabetes, good health care benefits had been crucial.

He stood, reeling his thoughts back to the present. "Why don't we save this conversation for another day and stay focused on Mrs. Francie right now, okay?" Perhaps Gloriana would be gone by then and the whole thing would be a moot point.

"Yeah, you're right." His daughter looked past him to the older rancher pacing beneath a large live oak at the center of the circular drive. "She seemed better when Mr. Krenek got here. They're so cute together." Ky got that wistful look in her eyes, the same one her mother used to have when she'd watch those sappy rom coms. How he wished Barbie were here now to see what a stellar young lady Ky had grown into. They'd gotten the cream of the crop when they adopted her as an infant. If only there could have been more.

"Judging by the look on Francie's daughter's face, I'm pretty sure she wasn't aware of the relationship between Francie and Bill." Perhaps if she'd come home more often— Wait, what was he thinking? Not with Ky looking at the woman as though she was the key to her barrel-racing success.

His main phone—as opposed to the one that was strictly for Ky and his folks—rang, and he pulled it from the clip on his belt to see Patty Hrcek's name on the screen. "Speaking of Mrs. Patty…" He placed the phone to his ear. "What's up?"

"Bad news, I'm afraid."

Anxiety tightened his gut as he moved to the edge of the porch. "How so?"

"My husband accepted a job at a ranch in Midland. We're moving in ten days."

"That's awful quick." Despite the calm in his voice, his mind was reeling. How was he going to find another coach for Ky this late in the game?

"They want him to start in two weeks. We figure we'll need a few extra days to get there, get our house set up and whatnot."

"Sounds like you've got a busy week ahead of you." With no time to spare for his daughter.

"I'm afraid so. But I still wanna squeeze in one last lesson with Kyleigh so we can say our goodbyes."

"If you have time, that'd be great." He eyed Francie's rosebushes, bursting with buds. "But I don't want you stressing over it." He'd be doing enough of that for the both of them.

"I appreciate that, Justin. I'll touch base with you in a day or two."

Ky was beside him when he ended the call. "What's wrong?"

"Mrs. Patty is moving to west Texas." He returned the phone to its clip.

Worry marred his daughter's usually carefree expression. "But who'll coach me?"

"She's going to give you one more lesson."

"That's not enough. The rodeo is still two and a half months away. I'm not even close to being ready to compete, Dad." Panic had her voice climbing an octave with each sentence.

"Calm down." He rested his hands on her shoulders. "We'll figure out something. We always do."

She heaved a sigh. "Mrs. Francie says God has a plan and a purpose for everything. That our job is to trust. So I'm gonna trust that God has another coach for me."

He looked at his daughter, wondering how her mother's death could possibly have been a part of God's plan. At least Ky had enough faith for the both of them, because Justin's faith died right along with Barbie.

After a long moment, Ky lifted her gaze to his. "Maybe Gloriana could help me."

His entire being recoiled. "While I know you would like that, I suspect she'll be gone even before Patty."

Her countenance fell, tearing at his heart.

"This is only your first year, Ky. You still have three more years of high school."

"Yeah, but there may not be another rodeo after this year."

He couldn't argue with her there. If this year's attendance was as disappointing as the last two, there likely wouldn't be any more rodeos in Hope Crossing. Meaning he'd better come up with one doozy of an advertising campaign to lure people in. But given that he knew far more about cattle than computers, he wasn't too optimistic—meaning his daughter's dreams were about to go up in smoke. Still, he'd do whatever it took to make sure that didn't happen, because there was no way he'd disappoint his daughter.

Gloriana might not be the same girl who'd hightailed it out of Hope Crossing and dreaded the thought of ever coming back, but there were a whole lot of people she had to prove that to. Including her mother.

With everyone gone, she joined Mom at the table. "Why didn't you tell me about the cancer? How come I had to hear it from Tori?"

"I didn't want to bother you. After all, you have an important job that keeps you terribly busy."

Shame had Gloriana hanging her head. That's exactly what she'd wanted people to believe. When she'd left Hope Crossing sixteen years ago, she'd vowed to make a name for herself, no matter the cost, and that drive had, indeed, taken her places. Only now was she realizing how high a price she'd paid, sacrificing relationships with her family and having no real friends except for Tori. And why she'd stuck by Gloriana all these years remained a mystery.

"Nothing is more important than you, Mom." Too bad it had taken Gloriana so long to figure that out. "That's why I'm here. It's time for me to care for you the way you always cared for me." She saw the skepticism in her mother's eyes, and rightfully so. The old Gloriana had a habit of making empty promises.

"I appreciate that, dear. I really do." Mom whisked a strand of her bottle-blond hair behind her ear. "But before you go makin' plans, there's something you need to know. About Bill."

Gloriana felt her cheeks heat. "I get it. You're both widowed and still relatively young. I don't blame you for wanting to go out and have some fun."

"Gloriana—" her mother's dark gaze bored into her "—Bill isn't just a friend."

Her chest squeezed. "Okay, *boyfriend*?"

"More than that." Mom clasped her hands atop her denim-covered lap. "He's asked me to marry him."

Gloriana felt her heart drop into her stomach. Not because her mother had moved on without Daddy, but because Gloriana had created such a chasm between them that Mom wasn't comfortable sharing the details of her life with her. "Wh-what did you tell him?"

"I told him I needed to think on it."

"That's good." Gloriana wished she'd have put more thought into her decision before running off to Vegas with Cody Donham after their freshman year of college.

"No, it's selfish. I love the man, but I'm afraid to commit to something I might not be able to see through."

Gloriana's anxiety inched higher. "What do you mean?"

Holding up a reassuring hand, her mother continued. "The doctors think the cancer is contained and that a hysterectomy will be all that's needed. But if it turns out they're wrong, well, I don't want to be a burden to Bill. Not after all he went through with Angie. She died of breast cancer, you know. Years of treatments and surgeries." Mom shook her head.

Gloriana hadn't known, but that didn't keep her from pretending she did. "Still, if he loves you…" She cleared the lump in her throat. "Whatever you decide, I want you to know that I'm here for the long haul. No matter how long that may be."

"What about your job?" Confusion marred her mother's beautiful face. Even in her midsixties, the woman still had flawless skin.

Gloriana shook her head. "It doesn't matter." Hoping her mother wouldn't press her, she pushed away from the table. "Those cookies smell delicious." She crossed to the granite-topped island and retrieved two from the cooling rack. "Chocolate crinkles. Yum." Returning, she handed one to her mother before reclaiming her seat.

Mom ignored the cookie and continued to watch her with a wary eye. "You worked hard for that job. It means everything to you, Gloriana." One brow hiked up. "Did you get fired?"

Naturally, Mom would assume that was the only reason Gloriana would come back indefinitely. Sadly, a few months ago, she would have been right.

"No. I requested an emergency leave of absence. When they turned me down, I quit."

"Gloriana!"

Retrieving a napkin from the holder in the center of the table, Gloriana set her cookie down and dusted the powdered sugar from her fingers. "Don't worry, there are plenty of up-and-coming newscasters ready to jump at the chance to host Nashville's top-rated morning show."

"Oh, Gloriana." Her mother crossed her arms and leaned back in her chair, scowling. "What would make you do such a thing?"

"Mom, I need to share something with you."

"A new job?" Hope had her mother inching forward again.

"No." Gloriana paused to gather her thoughts. "A few months ago, I gave my heart and my life to Jesus. He's changed my perspective on a lot of things. And while

I'm far from perfect, I'm trying very hard to be the kind of woman He's called me to be. A woman who puts others before herself."

Mom simply blinked. "I'd like to believe that, Glory. I really would."

"I understand your hesitance. I've always been a master manipulator." A skill she'd honed after realizing her good looks allowed her to get away with a lot of things other people couldn't.

"Well—" Mom lifted a shoulder "—I guess that's a start right there."

Gloriana reached for her hand and gave it a squeeze. "I've broken a lot of promises over the years, said things just because I knew they were what you wanted to hear without any respect for your feelings. I'm sorry."

Mom nodded. And though Gloriana knew the disappointment stealing its way through her wasn't justified, that her pastor had warned her trust wouldn't be easy for those she'd hurt, it was there, nonetheless.

Forgive me, Lord.

Releasing her mother, she looked her in the eye, almost fearful of how the woman might respond to the question she was about to pose. "Are you all right with me staying here? Or would you prefer…"

"Oh, honey, I'm going to need all the help I can get. What with the garden and the chickens, not to mention the house—"

"And you."

Her mother's shoulders slumped. "Yes, I suppose there will be that, too."

"You don't like asking for help any more than I do. Which is precisely why I'm here. So I can see to your needs, whatever they may be."

"I appreciate that, Gloriana." *But I'll believe it when I see it* seemed to be the unspoken words behind Mom's statement. "Now, you'd best tell Bill, Justin and Kyleigh to come back in here. They're probably worrying themselves sick."

"A lot of people care about you, Mom." Gloriana stood and pushed in her chair, trying to ignore the regret that threatened to strangle her. "I'll be right back." She moved through the family room, noting her old rodeo memorabilia lining the bookshelves, thankful Mom was at least comfortable with her staying at the house. While Tori would have welcomed her, being here would give her mother an opportunity to see just how much Gloriana had changed.

At least she hoped so.

When she opened the front door, three sets of eyes jerked to hers. "Y'all are free to come on in."

Bill wasted no time whisking past her. Obviously a man on a mission. How wonderful it must be to have someone love you that deeply.

Stepping onto the porch, she looked at the ranch manager and his daughter still lingering near the rocking chairs. "Justin, right?"

"Yes. And Kyleigh." He motioned to the girl.

Gloriana couldn't help smiling. "That one I remember." Her gaze darted between the two. "I owe you an apology for my behavior earlier. Concern for my mother had me a little rattled. However, I appreciate your desire to protect her."

His gaze narrowed. "Francie's done a lot for Ky and me. There's not much I wouldn't do for her." For a moment, she wondered why he hadn't included his wife, then she remembered her mother saying he was a widower.

Shifting her focus to his daughter, she said, "By the way, the cookies were delicious. Nice and soft, just the way I like them."

The girl smiled. "Me, too. Your mom told me to always set the timer for the shortest amount of time to make sure they don't get crunchy."

"That's the secret to a soft cookie." Not that Gloriana ever baked anymore. Perhaps she could brush up on her skills while she was here.

"I'm a barrel racer, by the way." Kyleigh's excitement seemed tempered with a hint of trepidation. "Just like you were."

"Really?" Gloriana's riding days had been some of the best of her life, thanks to Clay Gibbons. The retired rodeo champ had believed in her like no one before or since. He'd pushed her, making her work hard, teaching her to trust her instincts and believe in herself. Things that had served her well as she moved into the broadcasting world. "Are you planning to compete in the rodeo?"

"Mmm-hmm." Kyleigh nodded eagerly. "This'll be my first one."

"Now, Ky, don't go bothering Ms. Prescott. She's a busy lady." The challenge in Justin's blue-green eyes told Gloriana he'd heard enough about her past to have already drawn his own conclusions about her.

"Oh, don't be silly. I love talking rodeo." Waving him off, she gave his daughter her full attention. "You know, a couple of years ago I had the privilege of interviewing some of the top barrel racers in the country at the National Finals Rodeo in Las Vegas."

The girl's face lit up. "That must've been *so* cool."

"It was *very* cool." Looking back, Gloriana wished she'd considered going into the pro rodeo world. She'd had the talent, but her sights were set on college and television. After all, what better way to prove you'd made it than to have people invite you into their homes on a daily basis? "You know, a lot of those young ladies started out in local rodeos just like you and me. Matter of fact, Mandy Brinkman grew up in the next county."

Kyleigh's dark eyes went wide. "She's awesome! Do you know her?"

"We keep in touch. I'd always invite her to be on my show whenever she was in Nashville."

The girl looked at her father. "Dad, if we could get Mandy Brinkman to come to Hope Crossing's rodeo, people would come from all over. It would be so successful that they'd *have* to have the rodeo next year."

Gloriana struggled to grasp what the girl was saying. "Why wouldn't they have the rodeo next year?"

Hands on his hips, the cowboy cast his daughter a slightly annoyed look. "Ky—"

Undeterred, she continued. "They say there's no interest. That people aren't coming like they used to. But my dad's in charge of advertising this year, so I'm sure it'll be much better."

"Your dad is into advertising, is he?" Gloriana shifted a doubtful gaze toward the seemingly chagrined cowboy. "And just what do you have planned to draw in the crowds?"

Brow puckering, he glared at her. "Ky, why don't you go inside and start cleaning the kitchen for Mrs. Francie? I'll be in shortly."

The girl hesitated, looking from her father to Gloriana and back.

"*Now*, Ky."

Hanging her head, his daughter shuffled to the door and closed it behind her.

Meanwhile, Justin glared at Gloriana. "With all due respect, I don't need you coming in here and filling my daughter's head with all sorts of fanciful notions."

"Respect? Oh, please. You think you know me because of the countless stories you've, no doubt, heard. And while I'm sure you've probably lived a virtuous life, what I'm more interested in right now is the rodeo. Clay Gibbons poured his life into building that event, giving kids in rural communities a chance to test their skills. He's why there's a Lone Star Junior Rodeo Association that sponsors similar events all across the state. So why would they shut down the granddaddy of them all?"

He shrugged. "People aren't coming."

"That doesn't make any sense. The barbecue cook-off alone brings in crowds because the Hope Crossing Fair and Rodeo is a part of their big annual circuit. People come from across the state."

"I'm not aware of any cook-off and know nothing about Clay Gibbons's involvement with the rodeo. What I do know is that if we don't have a big turnout this year, the rodeo association is going to pull Hope Crossing from the circuit. And without their sponsorship, the event will be a thing of the past."

"Then I certainly hope you have an extensive promotional campaign in the works, otherwise I might be forced to step in and help you."

His face contorted. "What makes you think I'd let you do that?"

Taking a step closer, she said, "Because, like Clay, I know how to generate interest that will capture people's attention and draw them in."

He shifted from one booted foot to the next, glaring at her. "Well, maybe if you'd come back to Hope Crossing more often, you'd've known about the rodeo's decline. But you didn't care enough about your mama or the rodeo to do that. So, no, thank you."

A sharp retort was ready to fly off the tip of Gloriana's tongue but something—make that Someone—held her back. Just as well, she supposed. If she hoped to save the rodeo, she was going to have to prove herself to Justin. And that held about as much appeal as walking barefoot through a briar patch.

Chapter Two

Justin should have stayed in bed. If he'd had any inkling how this morning would unfold, that's exactly what he would have done.

It wasn't as though he'd had big plans. Getting the south hay meadow plowed before rain moved in later this afternoon was his only priority. That was, until his harrow began misbehaving. Yet while the problem was simply a missing pin that held one of the discs in place, the absence of a spare had him walking his last row to try and find it. That was when Ky had called to tell him about Francie. And he certainly hadn't planned to go toe-to-toe with Francie's daughter.

Pulling into the parking lot of Plowman's Feed Store, he shook his head. The only reason Ky wasn't with him now was because Francie had insisted they still had more baking to do. Prior to her episode this morning, they'd been talking about pies and even bread. He appreciated Francie's willingness to keep his daughter occupied while he worked. And teaching her life skills along the way was even better. He just didn't want Ky spending too much time around Gloriana.

He puffed out a laugh. Did she really think he'd be so flattered as to jump on her offer to help him? So he didn't know anything about advertising. He could take to the internet just as readily as anyone else.

You'd better get busy, then, because time is running out.

With a groan, he parked and stepped out of his truck, eyeing the gray clouds to the northwest. Looked as though the rain might be moving in sooner than expected. They could certainly use it. But he'd better get a move on.

At least Plowman's was one of those stores that carried a little bit of everything, because, in addition to the index pin, he also needed to grab some chicken feed for Francie, a much-needed Dr Pepper for himself and a can of coffee. And as he eyed the list of lunch specials taped to the entrance door, he decided chicken-fried steak fingers sounded like a good idea, too. The new gate for one of the pastures would have to wait until his next trip, though.

Inside, he beelined for the coffee aisle, almost running into Charlene Lockhart, president of the fair and rodeo board.

"Hey, watch where you're—" Meeting his gaze, her annoyance quickly morphed into a smile. "Oh, hi, Justin."

"Sorry about that." Out of habit, he touched the brim of his hat.

Clad in a pair of too-short cutoffs and a bright pink T-shirt with Rodeo Girl emblazoned on it in curly white letters, she gripped a gallon of milk with one hand and waved him off with the other. "No, I wasn't paying attention. I was distracted by these tiny stuffed animals." She picked up a fuzzy pink pig from the endcap. "Aren't they cute? My little Danica would love these."

Her "little" Danica was only a couple of years younger than Ky. "Where is your daughter?"

"It's her daddy's weekend." She continued to riffle through the miniature animals. "I didn't see an ad for the rodeo in this week's newspaper. I'm assuming you're planning to do that soon?"

"Yes." Though that was about the extent of it. "And Ky and I plan to have flyers all around town by the end of next week."

Abandoning the plush critters, she tucked her long, light blond waves behind one ear, her blue eyes meeting his. "I'd be more than happy to help you." The words all but dripped from her pink lips.

"Aw, that's not necessary. Ky and I have got things covered."

The electronic bell over the door dinged behind him, and Charlene liked to have strained a neck muscle trying to see whoever was coming or going.

Suddenly, her grin evaporated, and her body went rigid.

"What is *she* doing here?" Charlene looked downright disgusted.

Turning, he saw Gloriana surveying the place. "She arrived this morning." He knew the moment she spotted them.

She nodded and started their way. "Charlene, how are you?"

The blonde stepped forward to hug Gloriana. Something Justin found rather strange, given her obvious disdain for the woman.

"I'm just wonderful." Charlene released her and took a step back, a forced smile firmly in place. "Busy as ever. Between my daughter, work—the real estate business is booming—and serving on the rodeo board, I'm just a busy little bee." Her sudden euphoria had Justin lifting a brow.

"Well, you look great." There was no discounting the sincerity in Gloriana's tone.

"Oh." Charlene waved off the comment. "I'm a bit of a mess today, running around in this heat." She began fanning herself with her free hand.

Gloriana glanced in Justin's direction before shifting back to Charlene. "Actually, I'm glad I ran into you." She clasped and unclasped her hands as if she was nervous. Not at all like the woman who'd had no problem challenging him outside her mother's house. "I owe you a long-overdue apology, Charlene."

Perplexed, Charlene said, "Whatever for?"

Gloriana's gaze remained riveted to the woman. "Prom. I asked Lane to go with me after y'all broke up simply to spite you. That was wrong, and I'm very sorry for hurting you like that. I'm just glad you two found your way back together." She paused for a breath. "How long have y'all been married now?"

Squaring her shoulders, Charlene jutted her chin out, fire sparking in her eyes. "We divorced a year and a half ago."

A look of horror flitted across Gloriana's face. Her hazel eyes went wide. "I—I had no idea. I'm so sorry."

"No, you're not." Heat radiated from Charlene. "You had no intention of apologizing. You just wanted to rub salt in the wound."

"No, that's not true, Charlene. I promise, I did not know." She looked from Charlene to Justin, as if searching for help. "Please, believe me."

The blonde puffed out a sardonic laugh. "And why

would I do that? All you've ever done is try to make my life miserable."

Eager to remove himself from the drama, yet too stunned to walk away, Justin watched as Gloriana calmly drew in a breath and regained her composure.

"I'm sorry you feel that way, Charlene. Now, if you'll excuse me, my mother needs more butter." She whisked past them while Charlene glared after her.

"Can you believe that?"

As much as he hated to admit it, he kinda did. "It takes a lot of gumption to own up to our past mistakes." Even if it did seem rather odd. Made him wonder if Gloriana was on some kind of personal journey, trying to ease her conscience by coming home to her mother, apologizing out of the blue for a long-ago slight.

Shaking his head, he tossed the notion aside. He had enough on his mind.

"Oh, and trust me, Gloriana Prescott has *plenty* of those." Charlene's face grew redder by the second. "You'll have to excuse me. I need to get out of here before I blow a gasket." With that, she turned on her flip-flop–adorned heel and darted for the checkout counter.

Fine by him. Charlene made him nervous. She was nice enough—to him, anyway—but she never seemed genuine. Of course, after that nasty breakup with her cheating husband, that could be a protective measure, so people wouldn't see her pain. Justin could relate to that. He'd been covering plenty since Barbie died, caring for his daughter, losing himself in his work. Truth was, if it wasn't for Ky, he'd work even more. Home was just a reminder of what he'd lost. And how he could have prevented Barbie's death.

"Justin?" The sound of Gloriana's voice made him cringe. He wasn't ready for another round with her.

Reluctantly, he turned to face her. "Look, Gloriana—"

"I apologize for trying to insinuate myself earlier regarding the rodeo. It's just that the rodeo means a lot to me, so hearing it's on its last leg threw me for a loop. I really would do anything to save it, but you have your assignment and I'm sure you're capable of handling things on your own."

He wasn't anywhere near capable, but he wasn't going to admit that to her.

"That said," she continued, "I'm here indefinitely. For however long my mother needs me. So if you have any questions or need help with anything, you know where to find me."

Indefinitely? Great. That meant Ky would continue to pester him about Gloriana helping with her training. Though, looking at the woman before him, in her ultra-feminine white blouse and flawless makeup, he doubted she'd have any interest in getting dirty in the horse arena.

That suited him just fine. Despite her seemingly heart-felt apology to Charlene, he was still skeptical. What would prompt her to offer that apology after all these years, anyway? Unless it was just for show. She was used to being in front of a television camera; perhaps she'd honed her acting skills.

"I appreciate the offer. Now, if you'll excuse me, I have work to do."

Over the past few months, Gloriana had grown to love and appreciate Sunday morning worship service in ways she'd once thought impossible. But that had been back in Nashville. Now, as she accompanied her mother into the steepled beige brick building that was home to Hope Crossing Bible Church, her euphoria was tempered by a mountain of trepidation.

When she saw Charlene at the store yesterday, Gloriana recognized what she had to do. Sure, the setting hadn't been ideal, but she knew in her heart that God had placed Charlene in her path for a reason. Just the first of many apologies she had to make. She'd never imagined it could go so horribly wrong, though. The venom in Charlene's tone had rattled Gloriana to her core. And she wasn't one to rattle easily.

Funny thing was, she understood Charlene's pain. When Cody walked out on Gloriana after only four months of marriage, the ache she'd felt was almost more than she could bear. Throw in a good dose of hormones thanks to pregnancy, and she'd been a mess. Even now, she could see the disgust in Cody's eyes when he'd told her he didn't want a baby. Their baby. That it would tie him down, ruining his plans for a career in sportscasting. As if other sportscasters didn't have families.

Pausing in the church foyer, she squeezed her eyes shut as though the move would erase her ex-husband's contemptuous expression from her mind's eye. *Lord, please help me make it through the service without incident.*

"Ms. Gloriana!"

Amid the chatter of worshippers and the aroma of lemon oil, she opened her eyes to see Kyleigh Broussard bounding toward her, dressed in an adorable yellow floral cotton dress topped with a short denim jacket, her chestnut hair falling in ringlets down her back.

Seemed Justin's little girl was well on her way to becoming a beautiful young woman. And while Gloriana didn't know the man, she suspected he probably wasn't too thrilled with his daughter's metamorphosis.

"Good morning." Gloriana smiled as the girl stopped in front of her with a friend.

"Hi, Mrs. Francie." Kyleigh waved briefly before giving Gloriana her full attention. "This is my friend Callie."

Gloriana nodded in the direction of the cute blonde wearing far too much makeup for a girl her age. "It's nice to meet you, Callie."

"You, too." The girl gave a shy snicker.

Looking at her friend, Kyleigh said, "Ms. Gloriana has her own television show in Nashville, *and* she's a barrel racer."

Gloriana couldn't help chuckling. "The barrel racing was a very long time ago, girls." Not to mention said television show no longer belonged to her.

Callie peered up at her. "Do you know Luke Phillips?"

Luke was one of country music's rising stars. "I've interviewed him a couple of times." Since he was also from Texas, a small rural community a couple of hours from Hope Crossing, they had a lot in common.

Both girls' eyes went wide.

"Is he as cute in person?" Kyleigh flipped her hair over her shoulder as Gloriana leaned closer.

"Cuter."

The girls all but squealed, making Gloriana regret having encouraged them. Not in church, anyway.

"Girls!" Justin approached, the scowl on his face making it easier to ignore how nice he looked in those dark-washed Wranglers with the sharp crease and the crisp white pearl-snap shirt. "This is a church. Keep your voices down."

Gloriana couldn't help recalling a similar reprimand

from her own father when she was about Kyleigh's age. Unlike Kyleigh, who seemed chagrined, Gloriana had only grown more defiant.

Forgive me, Lord.

"Oh, Justin, dear." Mom inched closer, looking the picture of health in a tailored royal blue blouse and a pair of off-white slacks. "Don't forget, you promised to join us for Sunday dinner."

Despite yesterday's incident and her surgery tomorrow morning, the woman still insisted on preparing a big Sunday meal. The pot roast was in the oven and the rolls had been left to rise before they departed the house.

"Are you sure you're up to that, Francie?" Justin glanced Gloriana's way as if looking for backup. "I mean—"

Mom promptly waved off his concerns. "Pish, posh. I'm fine."

"We made peach cobbler yesterday for dessert," said Kyleigh.

Justin smiled. "Well, in that case, I can hardly wait."

It took Gloriana a minute to realize she was staring. This was the first time she'd seen Justin without his hat. His close-cropped brown hair was slightly longer on top and swept to one side. Paired with that brilliant smile, the man was downright gorgeous.

Her heart raced as he inched closer, looking at her as though he wanted to say something. Instead, he offered a parting nod and motioned for the girls to follow him into the sanctuary with its stained glass windows and cushioned wood pews.

As her pulse rate returned to normal, Bill joined Gloriana and her mother and escorted them along the sand-colored carpet to the third pew from the front on the right-hand side. Right where everyone could see them. Tongues were sure to be wagging when word got out that Gloriana Prescott was not only in town, but in church.

If any man be in Christ, he is a new creature: old things are passed away; behold, all things are become new. The verse from 2 Corinthians was her constant reminder that she had, indeed, changed. Now if she could just prove it to everyone in Hope Crossing.

She dared a quick glance toward the back of the church. When she'd texted Tori last night, her friend had said she was coming. Of course, she also had a three-year-old son to get out the door, a challenge for anyone, but even more so for a single mother. Tori's husband had been killed a year ago while serving overseas with the marines. Fortunately, Tori and her son were living in Hope Crossing at the time, so she had the support of friends and family.

Mom reached over and patted Gloriana's hand. "It's good to have you here with me."

She smiled at the woman who'd poured her life into her family. "It's good to be here."

As the piano began to play a few minutes later, Tori slipped past Bill and Mom with Aiden in tow, pausing to hug Gloriana before taking a seat beside her.

"Sorry I'm late." Tori, the quintessential girl next door, swiped her long blond hair behind her ear, her pretty blue eyes sparkling.

Joy bubbled inside Gloriana as she reached for her friend's hand. "I'm so happy to see you again."

When they stood to sing, the words of the hymns washed over Gloriana like a healing balm. In the midst of praise, she was free from her past. Until she allowed her gaze to wander. That's when she spotted Brady James at the opposite end of the pew. A good guy whose life she'd almost ruined.

No longer the timid teen with shaggy hair, he stood tall, looking confident with penetrating ocean eyes and thick, neatly trimmed brown hair that had been slicked back.

Gloriana gripped the pew in front of her until her knuckles turned white, gulping for air. She'd promised God and herself that she would make amends for all the wrong she'd done, but Brady was going to be the most difficult of all. He might not want to hear her out, and she wouldn't blame him. Not after she'd let him take the blame for something she'd instigated while she got off scot-free. Yet even though he'd been expelled from school, he never implicated her. He was a true friend. While she'd been a rat.

His presence had her fretting all the way through the pastor's sermon on the prodigal son. In some ways, she could relate to that younger brother. He probably imagined things would be bigger and better away from his father's estate. Perhaps he'd lived in his brother's shadow and wanted to be his own person. Yet while Gloriana had never starved physically, spiritually she'd been wasting away for years and had squandered relationships with those who loved her. And she'd given away the child she'd loved more than anything else in this world, not because she didn't want the precious baby girl, but because, as a divorced twenty-year-old college student, she knew she couldn't give her the life she deserved, with a mother and a father who both loved and wanted her and could provide for her.

Tears pricked the backs of Gloriana's eyes as the closing song began to play. She stood, quickly blinking them away and thanking God for bringing her home. At least until Mom was well.

"I'm so glad you're here." Tori hugged her again as soon as they were dismissed.

"Me, too." After a final squeeze, Gloriana released her friend, glancing toward the dark-haired toddler still sitting on the pew, coloring. "Would you look at that little cutie pie." Save for the pictures Tori posted on social media, Gloriana had never seen Aiden.

"Aiden—" Tori lifted her son into her arms "—I want you to meet Ms. Gloriana, Mommy's bestest friend in the whole wide world."

Even though they didn't talk or see each other often, they always seemed to pick up right where they left off. Tori had been a rare constant in Gloriana's life. Too bad Tori couldn't say the same about her.

The boy clung to his mother, only daring the occasional glance Gloriana's way.

"He's definitely a Stallings." Both Tori's late husband and his brother had dark hair and eyes.

"That he is." Tori tugged his shirt over his belly.

"You're still coming for dinner, right?"

"You know it. Wild horses couldn't keep me from enjoying your mama's cooking." Tori set Aiden on the pew and gathered her things.

Just beyond her, Gloriana saw Brady look her way, his gaze narrowing.

Her heart pinched.

Tori straightened. "Please say you're staying for Sunday school."

Gloriana glanced at her friend, keeping one eye on Brady as he made his way into the far aisle and started toward the back of the church.

"Um, sure. Which class do you attend?" She scooped up her Bible as Brady continued his retreat.

Tori heaved a sigh. "The young marrieds. It's kind of weird sometimes, but the only ladies' class is comprised of widows over the age of sixty. So, having you join me in the young married group would be a real treat."

It sounded like a better option than tagging along with Mom and Bill. But first, Gloriana needed to talk to Brady. "Where do they meet?" She watched him disappear into the foyer.

"Three doors down from the nursery. There's a sign at the door, so you can't miss it."

Gloriana moved into the aisle. "Great. I'll meet you there." She started to follow Tori and her son up the aisle, as eager as she was reluctant to find Brady, when her mom caught her by the elbow.

"Are you coming to Sunday school with us?"

"Tori asked me to join her." She eyed the people mingling just outside the sanctuary doors, hoping to see Brady.

"Oh, good. I was about to suggest that." Mom adjusted her purse. "We'll meet you afterward."

"Okay." With that, Gloriana hurried up the aisle and into the foyer. Yet as she searched for Brady, she was met with many a harsh stare. Warranted as they might be, she had more pressing issues. She had to find Brady.

When she finally spotted him, he was almost to the door. She picked up her pace, her heart racing as she dodged an elderly couple. *God, give me the words to say.* She neared as he reached for the door. "Brady!"

He paused, his gaze colliding with hers.

"Please, I need to talk to you." Breathless, she stopped in front of him, wondering when he'd gotten so tall.

He considered her for a moment. Though her hopes were dashed when he said, "Sorry, there's someplace I have to be." With that, he pushed through the door, his long legs carrying him into the parking lot before she could formulate a response.

Leaving her feeling like the worst person in the world. Yet even more determined to say her piece. She'd have to find out where he lived and go to him soon. Today, even. Because she wasn't sure she'd be able to sleep until she delivered another apology that was long overdue.

Justin needed to talk to Gloriana. But with a handful of other people gathered around Francie's dining room table, the setting was less than ideal. In addition to Bill, Tori Stallings, a local schoolteacher and apparent friend of Gloriana's, and her son had joined them. Yet while the current conversation was lively, his talk with Gloriana was going to include a helping of humble pie.

Last night, he'd finally taken the time to put some much-needed thought into his duty to the rodeo. But aside from flyers and a couple of newspaper ads, he wasn't sure what else to do. So he ran his ideas past Ky, who quickly let him know how pathetic they were and proceeded to tell him they needed to advertise on social media. She then rattled off several outlets, none of which he knew anything about. In the end, he'd gone to bed frustrated, feeling slightly older than Methuselah.

To make matters worse, when he woke this morning, Gloriana's words were scrolling through his mind like news headlines at the bottom of a television screen.

I know how to generate interest that will capture people's attention and draw them in.

Yeah, he didn't know how to do that. Now he was

going to have to go to her like a dog with its tail between its legs and ask her for help. If he didn't, the rodeo would be no more, and his daughter would be brokenhearted. She loved barrel racing and could hardly wait to compete. The poor kid had tried several things over the years— dance lessons, band, soccer, softball... Yet nothing had clicked. Until he took her to the rodeo.

Since his father was a ranch manager, Ky had been around horses all her life, riding whenever they'd visit his folks. But it wasn't until they moved to Hope Crossing that Justin gave in to her desire to attempt barrel racing. And it might just be the proud father in him, but the girl was good. So he wanted to nurture her passion. Even if it meant he had to bow to Gloriana Prescott. Because he would not let his daughter down the way he had Barbie.

"Well, as much as I hate to say this, I think we'd best be going." Her son sitting in her lap, Tori wiped his mouth, despite his protest. "Somebody is ready for his nap." She set the napkin atop her now-empty plate. "This has been so lovely, though. Thank you for inviting us, Francie."

"You're welcome. It's been fun to catch up with you." She reached over and tickled Aiden. "This little one is just too adorable."

The boy threw his head back then and whimpered.

Tori pushed her chair back. "Not when he's tired." She reached for her plate.

"Don't worry about that, Tori." Francie waved her off. "I can get them."

"Oh, no, you don't." Gloriana stood. "This one's on me. You sit and enjoy your company."

Beside Justin, Ky's phone dinged. A moment later, she looked at him. "Callie wants to know if I can come over for a couple of hours. They're on their way back from Brenham, so her mom said they can stop and pick me up. Please, Dad?"

Normally, Sunday afternoons were when the two of them hung out together. But since he was hoping to talk with Gloriana— "I suppose that'd be okay. Just this once."

Jumping to her feet, she threw her arms around his neck. "Thank you, thank you, thank you." She texted her friend back. Seconds later, she said, "They'll be here in twenty minutes. Can you run me to the house so I can change?"

That meant he'd have to come back to speak with Gloriana. Though he supposed it would give him the opportunity to change out of his Sunday duds, too.

"Okay, but we need to take our dishes to the kitchen first." Gloriana started to object, but he cut her off. "We've got this."

After thanking Francie for the wonderful meal, they hopped into his truck and headed down the gravel drive, winding past the horse barn and arena, the covered pens and equipment barn, into the woods until they reached the three-bedroom log-sided home that had once been Francie's husband's hunting cabin. Of course, when Boyd Prescott was alive, they hadn't needed a ranch manager.

By the time Ky left with Callie, Justin had changed clothes and had begun pacing the front porch, trying to decide how best to approach Gloriana. No matter what, he was going to look inept, so he might as well get it over with.

The return trip to Francie's moved at a more leisurely pace. He'd rather be doing just about anything but groveling in front of Gloriana. That fishing hole behind the cabin had been calling his name all week. Maybe he'd have time later.

A warm breeze carried the scents of earth and sunshine through the open windows of his truck as he approached the house. Tori's vehicle was gone, though Bill's F-150 was still in the drive. Since Francie's surgery was in the morning, Bill probably wanted to spend as much time with her as he could. Justin couldn't say he blamed him. Truth was, he envied the man. Bill had been given a second chance at love. Sadly, Justin had messed up so badly the first time around, failing the woman he'd vowed to love, honor and cherish, that any hope for another opportunity was a waste of time. He didn't deserve to find love again. Because if it wasn't for him, Barbie would still be here.

He shook off the glum thoughts and eased to a stop in the circular drive. In the shade of the old live oak, he exited his truck and started toward the house, only to see Gloriana coming out the door. She'd traded the black skirt, pale pink blouse and black pumps she'd worn to church for a pair of faded jeans, a plain white T-shirt and jeweled black flip-flops, and her straight hair was pulled into a ponytail. An oversize purse dangled from one elbow while she gripped a set of keys in her hand.

"Did you forget something?" She continued toward him.

"I was hoping to talk to you." The afternoon sun beat down on them as he stopped in front of her. "Are you busy?"

Her smile faltered, her gaze narrowing slightly. "I was hoping to visit an old friend. What do you want to talk about?"

He sucked in a breath. *Here goes nothing.* "Advertising for the rodeo."

Cocking her head, she said, "I thought you had that covered."

"Let's just say I've recently been informed that flyers and newspaper ads are lame."

She seemed to stifle a laugh.

"And while I hear social media is the way to go, I don't know much about Facechat or Snapgram."

She did laugh then. "Obviously."

Forging ahead, he said, "When we talked yesterday, you seemed rather passionate about the rodeo."

"I am. Without Clay and the rodeo, I wouldn't have had the courage to follow my dreams. What I'm having a hard time understanding is what happened to it. Why did people stop coming? You mentioned the barbecue cook-off was out, but what about the dance? Hope Crossing has one of the oldest dance halls in Texas right there on the fairgrounds. Boot Scoot Saturday night was always a big draw for adults and kids alike."

"I remember going once the first year Ky and I moved here. But the last couple years they had Saturday night bingo instead."

"Bingo?" Her face contorted. "Whose brilliant idea was that? No wonder the numbers are down. So what *are* they doing?"

"The rodeo, of course, with mutton bustin' for the little ones. The cobbler and canning competition. Your mom has won her share of blue ribbons."

Shaking her head, she said, "Please tell me they still have the midway."

"Such as it is. A Ferris wheel, carnival foods, pony rides, a few games…"

"Who wouldn't want to give up a beautiful June weekend for that?"

Shaking his head, he let go a sigh. "I'm afraid I can't argue with you. But if this year's rodeo isn't a success, the association is going to pull their funding, and kids around here, including mine, are going to have their dreams squashed. And I don't want to be the one picking up the pieces, knowing there might've been something I could've done differently. So I'm asking for your help."

Her frown failed to encourage him. "Justin, I hate to say this, but if you want to reach people outside Hope Crossing, you're going to need more than just advertising. You need an extensive promotional campaign like Clay used to do. And that should have begun months ago. But then—" she shrugged "—that's kind of hard to do when the only thing you really have to advertise is the rodeo."

"Are you saying it's a lost cause?"

"Not completely." With her arms crossed, she tapped an index finger against her chin. "But it's going to take something big to bring it back to its former glory."

"Such as?"

"For starters, bringing the dance back."

"We'll have to talk to the board about that." And after what he'd witnessed yesterday, that wasn't going to be an easy feat.

Lowering her arms, she said, "I have no problem asking them. Who's the director?"

He nearly choked on his response. "Charlene."

Gloriana's face went blank, her mouth forming a perfect O. "I see."

"I guess that's a deal breaker, huh?"

Her sudden interest in the grass didn't bode well. "No. However, we're going to have to approach her with an offer that's too good to refuse." She fell quiet for a moment before meeting his gaze. "I might have a couple of ideas, though."

He dared to hope. "Does this mean you'll help me?"

"It means we need to get to work right now."

"Now? What about your friend?"

She hesitated. "It was a surprise visit, so they won't miss me. Besides, the clock is ticking on the rodeo, so there's no time to waste. We need to get to work now."

Chapter Three

∞

Gloriana eased into the high-backed, gray vinyl chair in her mother's hospital room the next day and watched Mom sleep peacefully. The doctor had met with Gloriana once the procedure was complete, letting her know that the surgery had gone according to plan and, from what he could tell, her mother was cancer-free. News that had Gloriana sending up a prayer of thanksgiving.

Now, as relief settled in and Mom's IV pump clicked and hummed, Gloriana's thoughts drifted to the rodeo. She and Justin had worked well into last evening, even after Kyleigh had returned, so Gloriana never made it to Brady's as she'd hoped. Yet while a part of her was disappointed, knowing it could be a while before she'd have another opportunity to visit him, she was pleased with the ideas she and Justin had come up with. Things that could breathe new life into the Hope Crossing Fair and Rodeo. Starting with a phone call to Mandy Brinkman. An endorsement from the barrel-racing champion would go a long way toward drawing more attention to the event. Unfortunately, Gloriana had to leave a message and was still waiting to hear back.

In the meantime, she'd been making notes, formulating a detailed plan that encompassed everything from promotion to the event itself, knowing that getting Charlene and the board to agree to Gloriana's help would be the first hurdle. Not to mention the biggest. Charlene despised Gloriana, so swaying her wasn't going to be easy. Not only that, but as director, Charlene's opinions carried a lot of weight, meaning the battle could be over before it even began.

Gloriana's phone vibrated in her purse beside her, stirring her from her thoughts. Retrieving it, she saw Hawkins's name on the screen. Since she'd left a message earlier, she'd been expecting him to call.

Not wanting to disturb her mother, who was still sound asleep, she moved into the corridor before answering.

"And how's my favorite brother doing today?"

"I'm your only brother. And it depends. How did the surgery go?"

She strolled along the light-gray-and-teal linoleum toward the elevators. "Textbook. Doctor believes she's cancer-free, but we won't know for certain until he sees the pathology report."

"That's certainly a relief."

"Tell me about it." Gloriana felt as though a giant weight had been lifted from her shoulders. "By the way, did you know Mom and Bill are dating?"

"No, but I'm not surprised. I suspected something was up when I was home at Thanksgiving. Bill kept coming by the house, but he always had some flimsy excuse, like wanting something from Mom's garden. The man could've fed a small army by the time I left."

Gloriana smiled, recalling Mom's insistence that Bill

had come by to pick up some spinach the day Gloriana arrived. "Well, evidently he's asked her to marry him."

After a long pause, her brother said, "Interesting. What was Mom's response?"

Gloriana continued toward the sunlit window at the end of the hall. "She says she's holding off until she knows for sure about the cancer. So, based on what the doctor said, I suppose it's only a matter of time."

"I wonder why she didn't tell us."

Looking out over the top level of the parking garage, she saw a little boy holding his mother's hand, tugging her across the lot. "I *know* why she didn't say anything to me." Because Gloriana had always kept her mother at arm's length. "But I'm surprised she didn't confide in you."

"I reckon I can't blame her. With both of us gone, she's probably lonely."

"Agreed." And it made Gloriana sad to think that she'd played a huge role in that, making her mother feel unwanted. "Hawkins, I'm sorry I haven't been much help to you over the years. I've been selfish, off chasing my dreams while you were forced to put yours on hold." After getting his engineering degree from Texas A&M and landing his dream job, Hawkins had given it up and returned to Prescott Farms to run the ranch for several years following their father's death. Until Mom insisted they hire someone so he could pursue the career of his choosing.

"It's time for me to step up to the plate." She sucked in a breath. "Starting now. I quit my job, so I'll be with Mom as long as she needs me."

"Quit? What got into you?"

"Jesus."

A long stretch of silence had her looking at the screen to see if the call had dropped. Finally, he said, "That's the best news I've heard in a long time, Sissy."

His use of her childhood nickname brought tears to her eyes. "Me, too, Bubba." She sniffed as her phone beeped. Looking at the screen, she saw Mandy's name. "Can I call you back, Hawk? I need to take this call."

"Nah, I gotta run, but I'll be in touch soon."

"All right."

"Love you, sis."

Blinking away tears, she said, "I love you, too." She quickly switched calls. "Hello."

"Gloriana, it's Mandy Brinkman."

Turning away from the window, Gloriana leaned against the sill. "How are you, Mandy?"

"I am beyond great. As a matter of fact, I've got a scoop for you."

Gloriana could hear the smile in the young woman's voice. Yet while she'd have been all over a scoop a week ago… "I can't wait to hear. Though I should tell you, I'm no longer a part of *Rise and Shine, Nashville*."

"Oh, no! What happened?" Concern laced Mandy's tone. After Gloriana briefly explained her departure, Mandy continued. "I think you made the right decision. And once you're ready to get back to work, I'm sure you'll be picked up right away."

"Well, thank you. I appreciate the vote of confidence."

"Always. Now, about that scoop." Mischief laced Mandy's words.

"Yes?" Gloriana tucked her hair behind her ear, her anticipation growing.

"I'm engaged."

"Oh, Mandy! That's so exciting. Who's the happy fellow?"

"Landon Hightower."

"Wait. As in championship bull rider Landon Hightower?"

"That's the one."

"I didn't know you two were dating."

"That's because we've worked very hard to keep things under wraps this past year."

Gloriana's heart swelled with happiness for her friend. "Congratulations! When's the wedding?"

"Thank you. No date yet, but I promise you'll be one of the first to know." Mandy let out a breath. "Now, what can I help you with?"

Meandering back up the corridor, Gloriana explained about the rodeo, knowing how important it had once been to Mandy.

"That makes me so sad," she said. "That rodeo was the high point of my year back in school."

"Mine, too." Gloriana scrunched her nose at the strong antiseptic smell emanating from a room that was undergoing cleaning. "Which is why I'm determined *not* to let it fail."

"You definitely have my support. Whatever you need. I can do a couple of videos and put them on my social media outlets, commercials, whatever you want. I'll tell Landon, too. He idolized Clay, so I'm sure he'll be more than happy to put in his two cents."

"That would be wonderful. Why don't you go ahead and do a demo, send it to me and we'll go from there?"

"Consider it done."

"Thank you so much, Mandy." Passing the elevators

again, Gloriana saw a nurse rushing into her mother's room. Her muscles tightened. "I'll talk to you soon."

Tucking the phone into the pocket of her jeans, she hurried to see what was happening. Inside, three nurses hovered over her groaning mother while Bill stood against the wall, watching helplessly.

She looked from him to Mom and back. "What's going on?"

The rancher's stormy gaze turned her way. "How could you leave her?"

Gloriana struggled to understand. "She was asleep. Hawkins called and I didn't want to disturb her."

"I found her on the floor." His face was red, and fear carved deep lines into his brow. "Thanks to you, her incision reopened."

Gloriana's throat thickened as she studied her mother. Her face was so pale. How could this have happened?

She checked her watch. She couldn't have been gone more than fifteen minutes. Mom had been sound asleep. Why would she try to get up?

"You might have fooled your mother," Bill mumbled, "but you're not foolin' me."

Gloriana dared to look at him, her insides twisting into a knot the size of Texas.

"You come back here, claiming you're going to take care of Francie, but you haven't changed a bit. The only person you care about is you."

"But—" She stopped herself from saying any more. Arguing wouldn't do any good. Bill had formed his opinion of her, and there was nothing she could do to change it. Her energy would be better spent praying for her mother, that she would be all right. And that Mom didn't share Bill's sentiments.

* * *

Under a blue sky, Justin drove another T-post into the ground at the edge of the Grand pasture Tuesday morning, feeling far more optimistic about the rodeo. After meeting with Gloriana Sunday afternoon, he'd found himself wondering why he'd ever thought himself capable of doing something that would impact rodeo attendance. He was way too old-school. Yet in just a few short hours, Gloriana had come up with ideas that were sure to transform a sleepy little rodeo into a major event. Ideas that went beyond promotion to things they could actually promote. Her passion was undeniable. Something the board members seemed to lack. Which could explain the rodeo's decline.

With a couple feet of the metal post sufficiently embedded in the earth, he lowered the tubular driver to his side and grabbed another post from the pile behind him. Hearing Gloriana talk about how the rodeo used to be had him wondering why things had changed. After all, if something wasn't broke, why fix it? Now it was almost beyond repair. That was, unless they could talk the board—Charlene, in particular—into accepting Gloriana's help. And after what he'd witnessed at Plowman's Saturday, going eight seconds on a bucking Brahma might be an easier task.

Perhaps the news that Mandy Brinkman and Landon Hightower had agreed to do some promotional videos would play in their favor. He sure hoped so, anyway. Otherwise, he'd be forced to find other options for Ky to compete next year. Leaving him with only one choice. He couldn't let the rodeo go down without a fight.

He paced off ten feet, then thrust the post into the ground as the rumble of a diesel engine drew near. Lifting his head, he spotted Bill's silver F-150 easing to a stop alongside the farm-to-market road, the passenger-side window rolled down.

"Welcome to the party." Justin tipped his hat back and moved toward the truck. "Don't s'pose you'd care to offer a fella some help, would ya?" Not that he wasn't used to doing it himself. Mending fence somewhere on the ranch was almost a weekly occurrence.

The older man moved his head left to right, taking in the near fifty-foot opening someone's vehicle had created in the barbed-wire barrier early this morning. A vehicle that had since been towed away. Thankfully, no one was hurt. Still, the fence had to be repaired before any cattle meandered onto the road.

"Let me guess—" Bill shifted his gaze to Justin "—someone took the curve too fast." He nodded toward the front of his vehicle.

"More than likely." Justin moved away from the truck as Bill killed the engine and got out, clad in his usual cowboy-cut Wranglers and a chambray work shirt.

Returning to the post that now leaned slightly, Justin straightened it with one hand and lifted the post driver he still held in the other as the man caught up to him.

"Why don't you let me do that?" Bill reached for the driver as a couple of vehicles whizzed past.

Only then did Justin notice the dark circles framing his friend's eyes.

"I could stand to blow off a little steam," the older man said.

From the looks of things, he could use a good nap, too. "What's going on?"

Gripping the handles on each side, Bill eyed the post

as he threaded the iron tube over it. Then gave the post a few good slams.

Since his friend had yet to answer Justin's question, he figured it best to let it go. He grabbed another post and silently walked alongside Bill until they reached the next spot and repeated the process without saying a word.

Hoping to improve the man's mood, Justin switched subjects. "When's Francie coming home?"

The older man harrumphed. "*If* she comes home, it won't be till tomorrow or Thursday."

Concern had Justin narrowing his gaze. "What do you mean, *if*? Is she having complications?" If so, they must've just happened, because Gloriana hadn't said anything in her text messages last night.

Bill glared at him with bloodshot eyes. "That daughter of hers liked to have let her die yesterday."

Justin's insides twisted. He knew Bill wasn't exactly a fan of Gloriana's, but that was mighty harsh. "What happened?"

"As usual, she was too wrapped up in herself to pay her mama any mind." Bill raised the metal tube, covered the next post and forced it into the ground in a few deft movements.

His stomach churning, Justin retrieved another post. That didn't sound like the Gloriana who'd kept a watchful eye on her phone Sunday afternoon. The one who'd mentioned more than once that she was worried about her mother.

"What did she do?"

The older man tossed the driver on the ground and lifted his straw hat to drag a forearm across his sweat-covered brow. "She was gallivanting all over the hospital, talking on her telephone, while her mother was lying on the floor."

Justin felt his eyes widen.

"That girl had no business leaving her mother alone like that. When I got there, Francie was sitting on the edge of the bed with her back to me, tubes sticking out of her while she swayed back and forth." He pressed his lips together, the lines in his tanned face deepening. "Next thing I knew, she was trying to stand. She collapsed before I could get to her."

The sickened feeling in Justin's gut intensified. Francie was like family to him and Ky, so he couldn't imagine losing her. "Is she going to be all right?"

"Tore open some of her stitches." Bill shook his head. "No telling how it'll set back her recovery."

A cow bellowed somewhere behind them as Justin set the final post, wondering why Gloriana hadn't mentioned the incident. She knew how much he cared for Francie. "Any idea why she was trying to get up?"

"Doctor said she didn't know what she was doing. Blamed it on the anesthesia. All I know is if Gloriana had been in that room like she was supposed to, the whole ordeal coulda been prevented." He picked up the driver, and Justin stepped out of the way.

Why would Gloriana leave her mother? That was why she was here, after all, to look after Francie. At least that's what she'd said.

Bill finished, his face red. "Just goes to show that girl still can't be trusted."

Justin winced. That right there had been the main reason he'd been so reluctant to ask Gloriana for help. Yet her ideas had seemed so promising.

While they ran the barbed wire in silence, Justin's

mind continued to whirl. What if he and the board entrusted Gloriana with the rodeo's success and she walked out on them the way she had her mother? The rodeo would fail for sure. Ky would be disappointed. And it would be all his fault.

"They're sayin' we might get some rain this weekend," Bill finally said as he cranked the come-along until the wire was taut.

"We could certainly use it." Justin secured the wire to the posts, suddenly more worried about the rodeo than the rain. And by the time the older rancher departed, Justin was wound up tighter than the barbed wire. He'd been so certain about asking Gloriana to help him. Now that certainty was evaporating quicker than their rain chances. Leaving him to question whether accepting Gloriana's help was what was best for the rodeo.

Chapter Four

Gloriana slipped from her mother's kitchen into the backyard late Thursday afternoon to tend to a few chores and, more importantly, escape. Since Mom's fall hadn't hindered her recovery, they'd allowed her to come home yesterday, and Gloriana had spent most of today caring for her and making sure she was comfortable. But now that Bill had arrived, well, it was better for Gloriana to make herself scarce. After their little confrontation at the hospital, she'd just as soon steer clear of him.

While he might love her mother, it was perfectly clear he didn't care for Gloriana. So, she'd hang out with the chickens, water Mom's plants and do whatever else she could find to occupy herself until Bill was gone.

Standing on the patio, she drew in a breath of surprisingly crisp spring air, making a mental note to open the windows and allow some of that freshness to permeate the house. She slid her hands into the back pockets of her jeans and surveyed the expansive yard that was enveloped by a low, split-rail fence reinforced with hog wire to keep the cattle out and the chickens in while still allowing a view of the pastures beyond. And if she stood in the right spot, she could even glimpse the pecan grove alongside the creek.

As a girl, she'd always loved their hilltop view and wondered why people would ever want to live in the city where buildings obscured the landscape. And yet she went on to spend more than a decade bouncing from one metropolis to the next.

Shaking her head, she made her way across the rapidly greening St. Augustine grass to her mother's garden that stretched along the right side of the yard. When it came to beautiful gardens, Joanna Gaines and Martha Stewart had nothing on Francine Prescott. Inside the white, wood-framed fence that was also lined with hog wire, raised beds were separated by gravel walkways and boasted leafy greens, cucumbers, peppers, tomatoes, beans and more, along with a bevy of flowers, including amaryllis, gladiolus and Gloriana's favorite, snapdragons.

Two black-and-white hens clucked their way toward Gloriana as she opened the gate.

"Sorry, ladies. You know the rules. No chickens in the garden."

Making a mental note to check the nesting boxes, she unwound the hose and turned on the spigot beside Mom's potting shed, trying not to let Bill's words get to her again. Because regardless of her brother's reassurance that Mom getting up was simply a fluke and her mother's insistence that Gloriana wasn't at fault, there was one thing Bill had said she knew to be true—if she hadn't left the room, Mom wouldn't have fallen.

Once the plants were watered, she returned the hose to its hanger and moved on to the quaint white chicken coop adjacent to the potting shed. Yet as she reached for the door, she heard voices. Voices that were soon followed by the unmistakable sound of hoof beats.

Deciding the eggs could wait, she crossed the yard and slipped out the side gate to see Kyleigh practicing her barrel racing in the arena. Even from this distance, Gloriana could tell the girl was a natural. The way she moved with her horse brought back such fond memories.

Gloriana wished she hadn't been so eager to dismiss her riding as simply something to occupy her time until she could make her break from Hope Crossing. Then again, looking back on her life, she wished she could change a lot of things.

Curiosity getting the best of her, she continued down the gently sloped dirt drive, rolling up the sleeves of her flannel shirt. Before she even reached the arena that was simply a large, sand-covered, pipe-fenced oval space, a familiar thrill skittered up her spine. She and her horse, Have Mercy, had been quite the pair. Sadly, saying goodbye to that beautiful brown-and-white tobiano had been the hardest part of leaving Hope Crossing. And by the time she returned at Christmas, Daddy had already sold the paint.

Now, she shielded her eyes from the sun, watching as Kyleigh maneuvered her sorrel quarter horse through the cloverleaf pattern. An older cowboy hat–clad woman stood off to the side, her folded arms resting atop the fence while one booted foot was perched on the bottom rung as she watched Kyleigh run the course. And while Gloriana didn't readily recognize the woman, there was something familiar about her.

Gloriana approached as Kyleigh finished. The woman spotted Gloriana then and motioned for her to join them.

Kyleigh turned, her smile wide. "Hi, Ms. Gloriana." She waved.

"You're lookin' pretty good up there, kiddo." Gloriana grinned as she neared, then shifted her gaze to the other woman, recognition dawning. "Patty Hrcek?"

"Gloriana Prescott. Long time no see." The woman who'd once coached Gloriana took a step closer, her arms wide along with her smile.

"I'll say." Gloriana moved into her brief embrace. Like Clay, Patty was one of the few people in town who'd looked past Gloriana's many flaws to see her potential and then pushed her to be her best. Not that Gloriana had appreciated it back then.

Releasing the woman, Gloriana met her faded green eyes. "I know I didn't say it then, so I'm going to say it now. Thank you for investing your time in me. For helping me grow as a rider."

Patty waved off the comment. "You were the one with the talent." She eyed Kyleigh as she moved her horse alongside them. "Kinda like this young lady." Looking up at the girl, Patty said, "Why don't you give it another go so Gloriana can watch you up close?"

Kyleigh's smile grew even bigger. "Okay." She adjusted her turquoise ball cap. "Come on, Pretty Lady." She aimed the mare away from the arena, granting her some distance to pick up speed before crossing the starting line.

As soon as Patty gave the signal, Kyleigh raced back toward the arena, her horse's hooves pounding against the sand. Crossing the starting line, she aimed for the barrel on the right. Rounded it with ease before moving to the barrel opposite. Her turn there was a bit wide, costing her time, but she sailed on to the barrel farthest from the chute, made the turn and pushed her horse until she'd crossed the finish line.

Patty stopped the clock and showed Gloriana the girl's time.

"Impressive."

"What was it?" Kyleigh approached as Patty read the numbers. Frowning, she said, "I've done better."

"And you will again," said Gloriana. "You'll also have worse. That's why training is so important."

"Yeah, but with Mrs. Patty leaving…"

Gloriana eyed the older woman. "Leaving? But you've been here forever."

"My husband took a job in Midland so we could be closer to his folks. We move next week." Patty looked from Gloriana to Kyleigh and back. "You know, Kyleigh knows the basics. She's got good instincts, too. She just needs some fine-tuning." She toed at the dirt with her work boot. "Kinda reminds me of you. Did you see how she went a little wide on that second barrel? That was always your nemesis, too."

"I remember." Gloriana had never practiced so hard in her life to try and overcome that. But, eventually, she had.

"How long are you going to be in town?"

Looking at Patty, Gloriana said, "Until my mom is recovered from her surgery." Longer if the board agreed to her help.

"Well, perhaps you could spend a little time out here with Kyleigh? Give her some tips."

"That would be so cool," Kyleigh was quick to interject.

Gloriana shook her head. "Oh, no. It's been a long time since I've done any riding, let alone racing."

Patty shrugged. "Clay always said barrels were second

nature to you. You get yourself on a horse and you might be surprised how quick it all comes back."

Gloriana looked from Patty to Kyleigh, wondering how Justin would feel about that. "I'll consider it."

The sound of tires on gravel had them turning as Justin's truck neared. He parked beside the barn before joining them. And the way his smile evaporated when he spotted Gloriana told her he wasn't exactly happy to see her there.

"Sorry I'm late." His gaze moved from his daughter to Patty. "Lesson over?"

"Pretty much," said Patty. "Though I still need to say my goodbyes."

"In that case—" he shifted his attention to Gloriana "—could I talk to you in the barn, please?"

"Sure." They hadn't had a chance to speak in person since Sunday. Perhaps he'd been in touch with the rodeo board. If the news was good, they could start running Mandy's video right away.

After saying goodbye to Patty, Gloriana followed Justin to the red metal horse barn. This was the first time she'd been in there since she got back, and the aromas of horse, hay and leather swept over her like a welcome breeze on a hot day.

"I'm surprised to see you down here." He turned to face her outside the tack room. "Aren't you supposed to be taking care of your mother?"

The hint of accusation in his tone had her squaring her shoulders. "Bill is with her."

"That's good." Pink tinted his cheeks as his gaze shifted to the rafters. "How is Francie?"

"A little uncomfortable, but happy to be home."

"Glad to hear it." He continued to look everywhere but at her.

"What did you want to talk to me about?"

Finally he made eye contact. Moved his hands to his hips. "Yeah, uh, as far as the advertising and such for the rodeo."

"What about it?" While she took a step closer, he moved back a step.

"I don't think I'm going to need your help, after all."

Her insides twisted. She'd thought they were past all this. "How can you say that? I mean, after all the ideas we discussed. No offense, but surely you don't think you can implement them on your own."

"I just think it's going to be too difficult to get the board to agree to your help."

"We're certainly not going to know if we don't try." Obviously there was more to his sudden change of heart. "I thought you were excited about all this. Especially after I told you about Mandy and Landon."

"I have no doubt their endorsement would greatly increase our numbers."

"So what's the problem?"

His nostrils flared. "I just don't think I can trust you to follow this thing through. I mean, you promised to be there for your mother and look what happened."

Gloriana froze. She hadn't said anything to him about her mother falling. "And just what, exactly, do you think happened to her?"

"Oh, come on. She fell because you weren't there."

Gloriana felt as though a horse had kicked her. "I suppose Bill shared that little bit of information with you, didn't he?"

"Doesn't sound like you're denying it."

And here she'd thought they were getting on so well. On Sunday, Justin had seemed to value her opinion. But he still didn't trust her. And something about that really bugged her.

"Doesn't sound like *you've* got the whole story."

"You're not going to tell me?" He crossed his arms.

"Why waste my time? You've already made up your mind." With that, she turned and hurried out the door.

Justin had put his daughter off long enough. He had to allow her to see Francie. In all their time here at Prescott Farms, they'd never gone more than a day or two without visiting with the woman. Now they were closing in on a week. And while he'd purposely delayed things out of respect for Francie and her recovery, today he was flat-out procrastinating.

Any other time, he would've replaced the dilapidated pasture gate during the week, while Ky was at school. But he woke up this Saturday morning bent on getting the job done today. All because he was a coward. After his confrontation with Gloriana a couple days ago, he wasn't too keen on seeing her anytime soon.

But, like it or not, the time had come.

Gray skies held the promise of rain as he wound his truck into the circular drive at Francie's shortly after lunch.

"We're only staying for a few minutes, Ky. I don't want to risk wearing Mrs. Francie out." Or having another run-in with her daughter.

Holding a plastic wrap–covered plate of the cookies she'd made while he was working on the gate, Ky reached for the passenger door with her free hand as he eased to a stop. "She'll probably be glad to have company. I know I would if all I could do was lay around."

Francie definitely was more the social sort. Still... "It's not like she has a case of the sniffles. She's recovering from major surgery, and her body needs to conserve energy in order to heal." That fall she'd taken could have set her back, too. He was still surprised the hospital had released her so soon. Something Bill hadn't been too happy about. Likely because it meant Gloriana would be her sole caregiver.

Thunder rolled in the distance as they exited the truck and made their way up the walk. Hopefully things wouldn't turn stormy inside the house.

On the porch, he rapped his knuckles against the wood and glass door and was surprised when Francie opened it a few seconds later.

Her face was void of any makeup, though her smile was still bright. "There you are. I've been wondering when you two were going to pay me a visit."

"I made you cookies." Ky held out the plate. "Chocolate chip."

"My favorite. You didn't have to do that." Francie's dark eyes shifted to him before bouncing back to Ky with a wink. "But I'm glad you did."

"Mom, who's—" Gloriana appeared behind her mother, a laundry basket tucked under one arm. Her hair was piled precariously atop her head, and her gaze bored into Justin. "Oh."

"Look, Glory, they brought me cookies."

"You can have some, too," Ky was quick to add.

Gloriana turned her attention to his daughter. "Did you make them?"

"Mmm-hmm." Ky's smile was wide, her ponytail bobbing with each nod of her head.

"Well," said Francie, "I need to get myself back into my recliner before Gloriana scolds me again, so, Kyleigh, why don't you bring those cookies and join me, please."

While his daughter disappeared into the house, Justin stood awkwardly on the porch, locked in a virtual stare down with Gloriana. "Am I allowed to visit with your mother, too?"

Still standing in the open doorway, Gloriana stepped aside and motioned for him to enter. When he did, he could almost feel the heat radiating from her. She was still upset with him. On the one hand, he supposed he couldn't blame her. They'd made a lot of progress last Sunday. She'd had some great ideas. Ideas that could really boost the rodeo's attendance. But what if she wasn't willing to see them through?

What if she was?

Didn't matter. He'd said his piece the other day. He couldn't work with someone he didn't trust.

"You can see yourself in. I have laundry to take care of." She tossed the door closed before disappearing down the hallway.

He made his way to Francie.

"Your daughter is becoming quite the baker, Justin." With a cookie in one hand, she motioned to the sofa with the other.

Continuing across the large oriental rug, he said, "That's because she had a good teacher." He sat, resting his elbows on his thighs. "How are you feeling?"

"Given the circumstances, not too bad, I suppose."

Circumstances? Was she referring to the surgery or the

fall afterward? The one that could've been prevented if her daughter had been there like she was supposed to be.

"Though I don't care for all this sitting around, feeling helpless." She took a bite of cookie.

"No, I don't imagine you do." Normally, you couldn't get Francie to sit still.

"I'm blessed to have Gloriana here with me, though. She's been so attentive, taking care of me, the house, the garden, the chickens." She chuckled. "It's like we've had a role reversal. She's the mother and I'm the child."

He narrowed his gaze, rather taken aback by the statement. "I'm glad to hear that." He'd hate to think Gloriana was leaving her mother to her own devices.

"I always knew my Glory was quite the go-getter." She reached for a mug on the side table to her right. "It's nice to finally see her in action for a change. Though I would prefer being able to work alongside her." She took a sip.

Ky sat in the matching recliner on the opposite side of the table. "You should see the ideas she helped my dad come up with for the rodeo."

Justin cringed. He did not want to go there now.

"Ah, yes. The promotion." Francie set her drink aside before turning her attention to him. "Gloriana told me all about it prior to my surgery. Sounds like you two came up with some excellent ideas that could really recharge things."

He clasped and unclasped his hands. "It was Gloriana who had all the ideas." And, apparently, she hadn't said anything to her mother about their conversation in the barn the other night.

"Well, with her being in the broadcasting field, it stands to reason she would have considerably more knowledge than you or me."

"That she does." Yet he'd sent her packing.

"Justin?"

At the sound of Gloriana's voice, he jerked. He could only hope she hadn't been listening in on their conversation.

Standing in the opening between the entry and the family room, she continued, "Can I talk to you outside for a minute, please?"

Uh-oh. He looked from Francie to Ky.

"Don't you worry about us," Gloriana's mother assured. "We'll be fine."

It wasn't either one of them he was worried about.

He pushed to his feet, albeit rather reluctantly, and followed Gloriana out the front door and onto the porch.

While he closed the door behind them, she settled into one of the rocking chairs.

She gripped the rocker's arms, her knuckles white as she studied the ominous-looking clouds. "I'm just curious if you've pulled a lever on any of the promotional ideas we discussed."

Crossing to the edge of the porch, he shoved his hands into his pockets and peered off into the distance. "No, not yet."

Lightning flashed on the horizon.

"Well, I suggest you get a move on, then, because the clock is ticking. Surely I don't need to remind you that if you fail and the crowds don't come, the rodeo will be no more."

Thunder rumbled as he turned to glare at her. "No, I don't need to be reminded."

"Good." She pushed to her feet and moved his way until they were toe-to-toe. "Because I saw Kyleigh practice. She's passionate about what she's doing and is giving it her all. So I'd hate to think you're willing to let her down by settling for a so-so promotion campaign that will lead to the demise of the Hope Crossing Fair and Rodeo."

Let her down? Those three little words felt like a verbal punch in the gut. He'd let his wife down when she'd needed him most. And he never wanted to feel that way again.

He stared at the woman in front of him, despising the realization that she seemed to be their only hope for saving the rodeo. Agreeing to work with Gloriana was risky, at best.

Not according to her mother.

They might not even be able to talk the board into accepting her help. Then what?

At least you'd be able to say you tried.

Turning away, he roughed a hand over his face as the wind began to pick up. He did not want to admit that Gloriana was right. But if he tried to do this himself, he was sure to disappoint Ky. And just the thought of that made him nauseous.

"I'd hate for that to happen, too," he finally said.

Behind him, Gloriana exhaled. "At least we can see eye to eye on something."

Recalling how Francie had raved about her daughter, singing her praises, he faced Gloriana again, the taste of humble pie bitter on his tongue. "Look, I don't want to see Ky disappointed—by myself or anyone else. After hearing what happened at the hospital, I was afraid you might cut out on me, too. But rather than talking things over with you, I decided it would be easier to just cut you loose."

Shaking her head, she looked away, but not before he glimpsed the disappointment in her eyes. "And people wonder why I never wanted to come back home." Her words pricked his heart.

"Look, I was wrong about a lot of stuff, but mostly for not voicing my concerns and letting you have your say." He moved in front of her as the thunder and lightning drew closer. "I want to see the rodeo revived, but I don't envision that happening without your assistance. So, if you're willing to give me another chance, I'd really like your help."

Arms crossed, she stared off in the distance as the rain began to fall. "What about the board?"

"Meeting is Monday at seven. And like you said, if we're going to convince them you're our only hope, we'd better be prepared to make them an offer they can't refuse."

Finally, she peered up at him. "Trust me, I intend to do just that."

Trust? He doubted that. But if making his daughter happy meant setting aside his skepticism, he'd find a way to rise to the challenge, because he would not disappoint Ky.

Chapter Five

Gloriana waited until five minutes after seven to arrive at the Hope Crossing Library, just the way Justin had instructed her. The board was scheduled to meet at seven, but Justin didn't want to risk anyone seeing Gloriana before the meeting for fear they wouldn't let her speak.

Now she sat in the parking lot, waiting on a text from him to let her know the coast was clear. She prayed, asking God to calm her fears and to allow the board to hear the message she had planned instead of drowning out the messenger.

Her phone vibrated in her hand. She opened the screen to see Justin's text.

Come on in and move to the hallway on the right. Wait there until I come and get you.

She sucked in a breath and emerged from her vehicle into the humid evening air as the sun drew closer to the western horizon. "Showtime."

While she'd never been nervous speaking in front of people, her stomach knotted as she made her way toward the single-story brick building that also housed the fire station and town hall. Charlene likely wasn't the only board member who loathed her.

Stepping into the small but open space lined with rows of shelves and infused with that indescribable library aroma, she followed Justin's instructions and continued into the hallway where she heard voices coming from a meeting room. She pressed her back against the wall and checked her watch—7:18.

"Justin, do you have an update on advertising?" Gloriana recognized Charlene's voice.

"I do," he began. "After much thought, I've come to realize that advertising isn't going to save our rodeo. That said, we have the potential for some big things that *could* draw large crowds. However, it will involve some cooperation on the part of the board."

"What sort of cooperation?" Charlene's voice held a note of skepticism.

"Listening," he said. "Keeping an open mind."

Gloriana heard his boots moving across the beige linoleum, and her heart raced. *God, I need You now more than ever.*

Finally, Justin poked his head into the hall and motioned for her to join him.

Murmurs echoed throughout the large room as Gloriana entered. She dared a glance at the almost two dozen faces lining the tables that formed a U shape near the front of the room. And recognized almost all of them.

Jake Walker had been a star football player back in high school. AnnaLee Greene had been Charlene's flunky since junior high. Connie Sue Miller was crowned the very first fair queen when Gloriana was just a little girl. Gabriel Vaughn was now a large-animal vet. And the list went on. But her heart thundered in her chest when she spotted Brady sitting to her far right. Even more so than it had last night when she'd stopped by his house while Bill was with her mother. Brady hadn't been there, though.

Charlene banged her gavel, seemingly trying to bring some sort of order to the room. When things fell silent, she said, "Justin, I know you're not from around here, but Gloriana has a bit of a reputation in Hope Crossing."

"I'm aware of that." Justin faced Gloriana with what seemed to be a reassuring smile. "So is she." Addressing the board once again, he continued, "But she believes in the rodeo and she's got connections, not to mention some really good ideas. I think you'll like what she has to say." He took a step back and motioned for Gloriana to speak.

Gloriana couldn't recall the last time she'd been this nervous. Not even the first time she was on television.

If any man be in Christ...

She squared her shoulders, confident she wasn't alone. God was with her.

Armed with her tablet, she stepped forward. "Thank you, Justin." She turned her attention to the board. "As many of you know, Clay Gibbons was passionate about two things—rodeo and kids. It was out of those two loves that the Hope Crossing Fair and Rodeo was born. Clay worked tirelessly to create a family-oriented event that people would look forward to. And he used his status as a celebrity to make sure people far and wide knew about it.

"Now, in no way am I qualified to take Clay's place. However, I do have some connections."

Charlene lifted a brow. "So you think you can come in here, spout off a few names and we'll all be impressed, is that it?"

"Not at all. This has nothing to do with me. I simply want to preserve Clay's dream because I believe in it. I lived it. Clay gave me and countless others, including some of you, the courage to push ourselves, both in riding and in life. And I want to preserve that for future generations. I believe in this rodeo, and so do a lot of other people."

She tapped the button on her tablet and held it up for the board to see.

"Hi, y'all. I'm Mandy Brinkman, PBR National Finals barrel racing champ. As a young girl, I used to dream of being a professional barrel racer. And the Hope Crossing Fair and Rodeo was where I had one of my first opportunities to compete. So I hope you'll join me there the first weekend in June for some fun, awesome competition and, just maybe, a few surprises. Trust me, you won't want to miss this one."

Gloriana lowered the tablet. "Yes, you heard correctly. Mandy has not only agreed to do some advertisements for the rodeo, but she is willing to join us, along with another champ whose name I am unable to share at this time."

Her muscles relaxed a notch as interest flashed in their eyes. She'd captured their attention.

"I would also like to suggest Boot Scoot Saturday Night be reinstated. After all, it's a shame to be home to one of the oldest dance halls in Texas and then turn it into a bingo parlor. I've taken the liberty of contacting another friend who happens to be available that night and has agreed to perform at the dance hall."

"And who might this *friend* be?" Charlene all but rolled her eyes.

"He's kind of new, but you might have heard of him. Luke Phillips."

Jaws dropped and eyes went wide all around the table. Except for Charlene's.

"Look—" Gloriana moved a few steps closer "—I know most of you don't like me. But if you all are as interested in saving the rodeo as I am, then you will take me up on my offer. In return, I will not only set forth a social media campaign that will include Mandy Brinkman, but I will see to it every media outlet in the state is aware of the Hope Crossing Fair and Rodeo."

Charlene continued to glare. "You do know that the fair is just a little over two months away?"

"Which is why it's imperative we launch this campaign now."

AnnaLee Greene threw in her two cents. "We don't have the funds for extensive advertising or to pay for someone like Luke Phillips."

"What I've proposed is more about creating interest than actual advertising. A few spotlights in some major markets will get people's attention. Mandy has agreed to share videos and posts across her social media accounts, which will, no doubt, lead to more shares than we can imagine. The best part is none of this will cost us a cent."

Silence reigned as the board actually seemed to contemplate her offer.

Finally, Brady cleared his throat. "Gloriana and I have not always been on the best of terms. However, after listening to her just now, it's obvious that she shares my desire to save our rodeo. Like her, I knew Clay and witnessed his unending desire to provide a springboard for rural kids interested in rodeo. So I motion we move forward with Gloriana's plan. Because, let's face it, what have we got to lose?"

"I'm in agreement with Brady, and I second his motion." Connie Sue, who'd also been Gloriana's tenth-grade English teacher, leaned forward, resting her arms atop the table while her gaze traversed every face around it. "We've lost sight of Clay's vision. Most everyone here benefited from his desire to encourage others and help them be their best. He believed in us when we felt like no one else did and pushed us to be better, not only as competitors, but as people.

"Kids nowadays need that more than ever. And I don't know about you, but I don't want to be the one to take that away from them."

Conversations erupted around the table.

Charlene banged her gavel. "All right, let's take a vote. All those in favor of implementing Gloriana's plan, please acknowledge by a show of hands."

To Gloriana's surprise, everyone except Charlene raised their hand. And she was certain Brady and Connie Sue's comments had a lot to do with the positive response.

When the meeting adjourned, a couple of people Gloriana wasn't familiar with approached her, offering to help any way they could. As they were exchanging phone numbers, she saw Brady slip into the hallway.

After politely excusing herself, she hurried out of the room and managed to catch Brady before he reached the exit.

Peering up at him, she said, "I owe you a long-overdue apolog—"

He held up a hand. "Look, just because I agreed with you in there doesn't mean all is forgotten, Gloriana, so save it. The only thing I'm interested in is preserving the rodeo."

With that, he turned and walked out of the building. Leaving Gloriana to wonder if she'd ever get the opportunity to speak her piece. And compounding the guilt she'd harbored for far too long.

Three days later, Justin was still trying to wrap his head around the fact that the board had voted almost unanimously to bring Gloriana onboard. And the woman hadn't wasted any time getting to work.

While Ky finished her homework, he pulled up to the barn in the utility vehicle early Thursday evening, amazed at all Gloriana had accomplished just since the board meeting. Mandy Brinkman and Landon Hightower were already promoting the fair and rodeo all over social media. Gloriana had interviews set up with television stations in Houston and Dallas, not to mention several more with country radio stations throughout the state.

The woman was a force to be reckoned with, all right. Meanwhile, he didn't have a single coaching prospect for Ky.

He'd contacted a couple of people but come up empty-handed. Both already had enough to handle, though one mentioned the possibility of squeezing Ky in a for a single lesson. That wouldn't do, though. His daughter was still building her confidence as a racer and needed someone to nurture the talent she already had. But around these parts, pickings were pretty slim.

Stepping out of the UTV, he eyed the sun hanging in the western sky. The fact that Ky had heard Patty suggest Gloriana coach her wasn't helping his case, either. His daughter had latched on to that tidbit and had been pestering him about it ever since, despite his continued reminders that Gloriana herself admitted she hadn't ridden in a long time.

He lifted his ball cap and shoved a hand through his

hair, wondering what he was going to do. He didn't want to disappoint Ky. But what if he couldn't find another coach?

The sound of hooves on gravel had him turning to see Gloriana approaching, atop Shadow, no less. Francie must have suggested Gloriana take the black mare out for some exercise.

"Nice day for a ride," she said as she approached.

In an instant, his argument about her not riding flew right out the window. He hated to admit it, but she looked good in the saddle. Like she was born to it. From her dingy straw hat right down to her well-worn Ariats, both likely leftover from her rodeo days.

He reached for Shadow's bridle. "First ride since you've been back?"

"More like first ride in years." That didn't stop her from dismounting like a pro.

"How was it?"

"Let's just say sometimes you don't realize how much you've missed something until you revisit it."

He couldn't help smiling. "That good, huh?"

"I'd forgotten how having the wind at your face can help clear the cobwebs from your mind." She gave the horse a pat. "I think Shadow enjoyed the workout, too. We wandered down by the creek for a bit." She looked at Justin. "It's running kind of low for spring."

"We're barely into April, but you're right. Our rainfall totals during the winter months didn't amount to much." He paused. "How's Francie doing?"

"Good. She had her post-op visit the other day, and the doctor was pleased with her progress. Though he was also quick to add that did not mean she was free to resume her normal activities."

Justin couldn't help chuckling. "Sounds like he's onto her."

Gloriana glanced around. "Where's Kyleigh?"

"Doing homework. At least, that's what she's *supposed* to be doing."

"Have you found a coach for her yet?"

He shook his head, silently hoping she wouldn't mention Patty's suggestion that she take on the role.

"That's a shame. Though I don't suppose there are many options around here."

"Nope." He scanned the horizon—anything to keep from making eye contact. He'd seen how determined Gloriana could be when she got an idea in her head, so he wasn't about to risk any sort of encouragement.

"I'll be praying God leads you to the right person," she said instead.

Though her words made him uneasy, at least he could take comfort in knowing Ky would have someone interceding for her. God hadn't heard his prayers the day Barbie died. Why would He listen now?

"Ms. Gloriana!" His daughter's voice mingled with the sound of boots pounding against gravel, announcing Ky's arrival.

While Gloriana waved, he turned to see his girl's smiling face. "Finished your homework already?"

"Yep." She stopped in front of them, slightly winded. "Algebra is easy."

Gloriana laughed. "That's funny. I always thought the same thing."

Justin looked at each of them. "What planet did you two come from? Nobody thinks algebra is easy." Focusing on his daughter, he said, "What are your plans now?"

"I thought I'd get in a couple of practice runs."

He checked his watch. "Better hurry, then. It'll be dark in an hour."

While Ky saddled Pretty Lady and took her for a warm-up run, Gloriana untacked Francie's horse and released her out to pasture while Justin got into place.

A short time later, Ky paused at one end of the arena. "You got the stopwatch, Dad?"

Standing outside the fence, flush with the starting line, Gloriana at his side, he held up his hand to reveal the timepiece. "I'm ready when you are."

Ky aimed her horse away from them and set Pretty Lady into motion. After picking up speed, she turned the animal and raced toward the starting line. As Ky maneuvered around each of the three barrels, Justin couldn't help noticing how intently Gloriana watched his daughter. The entire time, her gaze was fixed on both horse and rider.

Justin announced Ky's time when she finally came to a stop.

His daughter frowned from her saddle. "That's worse than my last time."

"Try tightening your core and hold it as you head into that first barrel," offered Gloriana. "See if it helps your stability."

Ky nodded and took off to repeat the process. Less than two minutes later, she rejoined them, her expression full of anticipation. "Well?"

Smiling, he looked up at her. "You shaved off point-three seconds."

"Yes." She pumped her fist in the air. Then, turning her attention to Gloriana, she said, "You were right about the stability. I think I need to work on my core strength, though."

Gloriana nodded. "It'll come."

Justin looked at his daughter. "You done or are you gonna go again?"

"I want to try one more time. I still don't like the way I head into that final barrel."

"Mind if I give you another suggestion?" Gloriana looked at Ky.

"Of course not."

"Snug your elbow to your side." Gloriana demonstrated. "Keeping it tight will make you less likely to lean."

While Ky rode off, Justin turned to Gloriana. "How were you able to pick up on those things? I mean, she looked just fine to me."

She shrugged. "Sometimes it's the little things that cost riders time. You'd be surprised the difference one little tweak can make."

And she was right. "Good job, Ky," he said when she approached them after her final attempt. "Are you ready for this?"

Her grin was full of anticipation.

"You shaved off another point-seven seconds."

Her dark eyes went wide. "No way!"

"Yes, way." He held his hand up for a high five. "You cut your time by a full point in less than an hour."

"See, I told you Ms. Gloriana would make a great coach."

Gloriana held up her hands, palms out. "No, no. I'm no coach. I was simply giving you a few pointers based on my own experience."

"But they worked." Ky couldn't seem to stop smiling. "I beat my record time."

She was right. Gloriana's tips had made a difference in

her performance, but Justin still wasn't crazy about the idea of his daughter spending a lot of time with someone he barely knew.

It's not like they'd be together for hours on end.

True. And he could always supervise.

He glanced at his daughter. Not only did she love barrel racing, she showed real promise. He wanted to nurture that. And in a very short amount of time, Gloriana had recognized issues Ky had been struggling with for months. She'd offered suggestions Ky could easily wrap her head around, and they worked.

You want her to win, don't you?

Winning wasn't everything. But he did want Ky to have the best shot possible. And since he had no prospects for another coach, perhaps it wouldn't be such a bad idea for Gloriana to work with her.

"The kid has a point." He dared to meet Gloriana's hazel eyes, noticing the flecks of gold around the iris. "Your input allowed her to have a faster race. I mean, Patty's always harping on Ky about her stability in the saddle, yet she still had a problem. You gave useful advice she was able to grasp right away."

Still atop her horse, Ky nodded. "Please, can you coach me?"

"Ky, you heard Ms. Gloriana." He looked at his daughter. "She's not a coach."

As the girl's shoulders sagged, he added, "But maybe we could talk her into observing you and offering some more suggestions." He glanced at Gloriana.

The woman's gaze bounced between him and Ky before narrowing slightly. "Hmm…sounds an awful lot like coaching to me."

"We're not asking you to do any more than you did

here today." Justin couldn't believe he was actually trying to talk her into this.

"Except…maybe more often?" Ky scrunched her nose.

Gloriana looked from Ky to Justin and back again. "With those pleading looks, how can I say no?"

While his daughter cheered, Justin suddenly realized what he'd signed on for. Not only would he and Gloriana be working together on the rodeo, now they'd be spending even more time together.

Chapter Six

"I can't believe my time actually increased." Kyleigh frowned as she untacked her horse that Friday evening. Good Friday. A day that, in the past, had held little meaning for Gloriana. This year was different, though. And as she'd read Luke's account of Jesus's crucifixion this morning, she was again brought to tears by the depth of His love for her.

"Point-zero-one is not that big a deal." Gloriana watched as the girl hoisted the saddle from Pretty Lady and moved it to the nearby rack. "You're working on improving your skills."

"I know." The girl sighed. "I guess I just got my hopes up after yesterday."

Gloriana lifted the curry comb from the hook on the wall and passed it to Kyleigh, recalling how Clay had always encouraged her. "Let's get one thing straight right now. You're going to have good days and bad days. It's best not to dwell on either one. Instead, just go out there and do the very best you can at that very moment."

Dark chocolate eyes met Gloriana's. "I did give it my all tonight."

"Then that's all that matters."

"Y'all finished?"

She turned to see Justin coming into the barn. While he'd planned to stay for the duration of Kyleigh's practice, he'd been forced to leave when Mom contacted him, saying someone had called about a cow on the road.

"We are." Gloriana took a step back while Kyleigh tended her horse, savoring the comforting aromas of the barn. "Did you find the cow?"

He nodded. "It wasn't one of ours, though. It came from the Blanchards' pasture across the road, but I got it back in, then notified them before stopping by Francie's to let her know." He smiled, shifting his attention to his daughter. "I have some news for you, young lady."

Kyleigh paused Pretty Lady's grooming to eye her father. "What is it?"

"Mrs. Francie invited us for Easter dinner."

Their excitement had Gloriana shaking her head. "Yes, despite her ongoing recovery, Mom still insists on hosting. However, I should warn you that it'll be yours truly preparing the meal, so now is your opportunity if you'd like to bow out."

"I could help you." Kyleigh bounced on the balls of her booted feet.

Gloriana knew the girl loved helping in the kitchen. Yet she also knew how her father felt about Kyleigh spending too much time with her, despite his seemingly increased tolerance of Gloriana. "You should probably check with your daddy first."

Arms crossed—a move that only served to accentuate his massive biceps—Justin glared at his daughter. "You should also wait to be *asked* to help."

While Kyleigh hung her head, Gloriana quickly caught Justin's attention and nodded her approval.

A moment later, he lowered his arms and lovingly touched his daughter's chin, urging her to look up at him. "But if it's okay with Ms. Gloriana, it's fine by me."

As the smile returned to her face, Kyleigh jerked a hopeful expression toward Gloriana.

"I'd welcome the help."

Practically bubbling with excitement, Ky clasped her hands under her chin. "What all are you making?"

"Let's see. Ham, onion shortcake—" Gloriana ticked the items off on her fingers "—Mom's favorite Jell-O salad with pineapple and cottage cheese, balsamic-glazed Brussels sprouts—"

"Ew…" Justin's face contorted. "You lost me at Brussels sprouts."

Gloriana shrugged. "Humph, too bad. Guess that means more for me."

"What about dessert?" Kyleigh's eyes were wide.

"I was thinking cupcakes would be cute, with little tinted coconut nests and jelly-bean eggs."

"I love that idea." The girl's smile was so big she looked like she might explode.

"And then, maybe, a lemon meringue pie."

"That'll make my dad happy." Kyleigh looked at her father. "That's your favorite, isn't it?"

"You know it."

Gloriana playfully eyed the grinning cowboy. "What a shame."

His confused gaze turned her way. "Why's that?"

"Mom always says no dessert if you don't eat your vegetables."

His brow furrowed as his hands moved to his hips. "I'm a grown man."

She shook her head. "Sorry. Mom's house, Mom's rules. You'll have to take that up with her."

"Wait." Kyleigh seemed to ignore her father. "What about deviled eggs?"

Gloriana feigned a face palm. "I'm so glad you reminded me. Yes, we have to have deviled eggs on Easter."

Kyleigh addressed her father next. "Are we still doing a fire tonight?" The girl could shift gears faster than a driver at the Indy 500. Still, Gloriana appreciated the way she reveled in every experience.

"It's all ready to go. All we need to do is light it."

"Did you get chocolate for s'mores?"

"Like I'd forget something as important as that."

Kyleigh's expression took on a hint of timidity then. "Could...Ms. Gloriana join us?"

Trying to spare Justin from an awkward situation, Gloriana pretended to look at her watch. "That's okay. Bill will be leaving soon, so I need to get back to the house." She moved toward the door, wishing she didn't have to go. "See you tomorrow."

With that, she exited the barn and made her way up the gravel drive as the sun began to set. Looking up at the cloudless sky, seeing the first stars to the east, she couldn't help thinking that this was, indeed, a perfect night for a campfire. The air was still and cool but not cold. Justin and Kyleigh were going to have a great time.

Bill's truck was still in the drive, and when Gloriana entered the kitchen, the delightful aroma of popcorn filled the space. Then she noticed Bill pulling a bag of popcorn out of the microwave.

"Hi, hon." Mom waved from the sofa in the family room as Gloriana closed the door. "We're just about to watch *Titanic*. Care to join us?"

Titanic? That was one of the longest movies in recent history. Why were they starting it now?

Her gaze moved back to the kitchen, where Bill poured popcorn into a bowl, watching intently as every kernel tumbled from the bag. Or simply trying to avoid Gloriana.

Surely he didn't want her hanging around.

Continuing into the family room, she said, "Thanks, but I think I'll pass." There was a TV in her room, so she could watch whatever she wanted. Though she could also sit down with her laptop and see what kind of feedback they were getting on the rodeo promotion. She'd been updating the fair and rodeo's previously dormant Facebook page at least once a day, trying to not only capture but hold people's interest. Any time there was momentum building, she did her best to capitalize on it.

Her phone vibrated in her back pocket. Stepping into the hall, she retrieved it to discover a text from Justin. It was a photo of an all-too-inviting campfire behind the cabin.

Gloriana bit her bottom lip. A campfire sounded way more fun than sitting in her room. But what if Justin didn't want her there?

Then why did he send you the picture?

She wouldn't put it past Kyleigh to have sent it from her dad's phone.

The device vibrated again. This time there was a message.

Nice night for a fire.

Gloriana's heart thudded against her ribs. Was that an invitation? If so, who actually sent it? She could just imagine showing up over there and seeing the surprise on Justin's face. Not to mention his annoyance as he re-alized what his daughter had done.

Thumbs hovering over the screen, she took a deep breath and typed. Much more appealing than watching Titanic with Mom and Bill.

Shortly after she hit Send, a bubble wiggled on the screen.

Sounds like torture. Why don't you join us?

Her pulse quickened. That was definitely Justin.
Another bubble, followed by—

Just have them text when Bill's ready to leave.

Her palms grew sweaty as she blew out a nervous breath. Which was completely ridiculous. It wasn't like this was a date or anything. Just two friends—no, wait. She wasn't even sure she and Justin could be classified as friends, despite the fact that they seemed to be getting along. Instead his daughter had probably coerced him into extending an invitation. One Gloriana was finding it hard to resist, no matter the circumstances.

She glanced over her shoulder into the family room as Bill settled beside her mother. Nope, this was too nice a night to be cooped up inside.

She sent another message.

On my way.

Justin wasn't sure why he felt compelled to invite Glo-riana to join him and Ky. After all, she'd come home to be with her mother. He'd had no idea Bill would decide to stay for a late movie.

Maybe it was simply because Ky had wanted her to stay, and he'd failed to extend an invitation earlier. Though it also could have been the look on Gloriana's face when she left the barn. A longing, perhaps, that made him think she wanted to stay.

Since when have you been concerned with what Gloriana wants?

Good question. One he wasn't prepared to answer. Not while she was pulling up in Francie's UTV.

He stood from his camp chair as she turned off the engine and stepped out of the vehicle.

"Your invitation was as timely as it was unexpected." Her long ponytail swayed from the back of her camo ball cap as she continued toward them. Dressed in a gray T-shirt, faded jeans and those worn Ariats, she looked like she belonged in the country.

Ky hurried from her own chair to greet their guest. "My dad felt bad for not asking you to stay. Said he'd hate for you to feel unwanted."

Justin cringed. Nothing like being thrown under the bus by your own kid. "I believe what I said was that I should have at least extended an invitation."

Ky sent him a funny look. "Yeah, that's what I said." She turned back to their guest. "I'm just glad you were able to come."

"Me, too." Gloriana slipped her hands into her back pockets, her gaze drifting to the blue and orange flames flickering inside the metal pit. "I've always loved campfires."

"In that case—" Justin motioned to the three camp

chairs positioned around the fire "—pull up a chair and have a seat."

"Don't mind if I do." She settled to the left of Ky and let out a contented sigh. "I've missed this." Tilting her head back, she stared up at the night sky. "So many more stars to see out here than in the city."

Embers sprang from the fire and danced toward the sky.

To the right of Ky, Justin followed Gloriana's lead and looked up. "I know what you mean. You kind of take the stars for granted when you grow up in the country."

"What time should I come over tomorrow to help you cook?"

Gloriana faced Ky. "We'll probably focus on the desserts tomorrow, maybe some prep—you know, chopping and such—for the main course, so we can either do it in the morning or after lunch. Which would you prefer?"

Ky shrugged, her smile wide. "Either one is fine."

"In that case, why don't you come by around nine."

"Okay." Suddenly his daughter bolted from her seat. "Want to see my Easter dress?"

"Sure." Gloriana chuckled as Ky disappeared into the house.

He leaned forward, resting his elbows on his thighs. "Sorry about that."

"Don't be." Gloriana waved him off. "I was the same way when I was her age. The annual Easter dress is a big deal, you know."

"So I've been told."

The wooden screen door on the house smacked closed a second time as Ky hurried their way, the hanger holding the bright pink dress dangling from one hand.

"It's kind of simple," Ky said as Gloriana stood to meet her.

"There's nothing wrong with simple." Gloriana took hold of the flared skirt and held it out for a better look. "Especially when it's such an eye-catching color. And I *love* the color."

"You don't think it's too bright?"

"Not at all." She looked at Ky. "With your dark hair and eyes, you're going to look absolutely stunning."

His daughter's face lit up like Cowboys stadium. "You really think so?"

"I sure do."

Ky let out a squeal. "I can't wait till Sunday."

Justin eyed the girl. "Well, if you leave it out here much longer, you're going to go to church smelling like a campfire."

"Good point." With that, she turned and hurried back into the house.

"Oh, to be young again." Chuckling, Gloriana returned to her seat. "You have one beautiful daughter, Justin."

"Thanks. I think so, too." Pride made it nearly impossible for him to stop grinning.

"Where does she get her dark eyes from? Her mother?"

"They're pretty, aren't they?" He shifted in his seat. "But it's anyone's guess where they came from."

Gloriana looked at him curiously.

"Ky was adopted." Clasping his hands together, he turned her way. "Barbie, my wife, had type one diabetes, making pregnancy too risky. We always knew we would adopt."

Her expression softened, and for a moment, it seemed as though her mind had gone somewhere else. "Kyleigh is a blessed little girl to have ended up with such wonderful parents."

He shrugged. "I just wish Barbie was here to see her now. That kid has a heart for God, just like her mama did."

Gloriana cocked her head, her gaze riveted to his. "And what about her father?"

He stared at his hands. "Ky has a lot of faith, and I don't want to influence her beliefs, but I always see to it we're in church."

"Okay. That's good. But what about *your* faith?"

Even though his gaze remained on the fire, he could feel the intensity of Gloriana's stare. "I used to be a lot more like Ky. Before Barbie died."

"I don't mean to be disrespectful, Justin, but what does your wife's death have to do with your belief in God?"

He leaned back, rubbing his suddenly sweaty palms over his denim-covered thighs, wondering what was keeping Ky. "I still believe in Him." He glanced her way. "I guess I just don't trust Him like I used to."

She studied him for a long moment. "I'm sure you won't find this too difficult to believe, but despite being raised in the church, I spent a lot of years running from God. So many people had let me down that the only one I was willing to trust was myself. Which, by the way, can be very exhausting."

He looked her way, wondering where she was going with this.

"A few months ago, I quit running."

"Because?"

She leaned back in her chair. "There was a pastor at this little church in Nashville I interviewed last Christmas, and I was so intrigued by his love for others that I ended up attending one of their services. Then another and another. It got to where I couldn't wait for Sunday, so I joined a ladies' Bible study." She paused. "Bottom line is, I met the real God. Not the authoritarian I believed Him to be, not a god who expects me to be perfect, but *the* God who loved me enough to pursue me even when I chose not to trust Him."

Anger wormed its way through Justin's gut. "That's great for you, but has He ever robbed you of someone you loved?"

"As a matter of fact—"

"I've got the s'mores stuff." The screen door closed with a bang as Ky started toward them, holding a tray filled with marshmallows, graham cracker squares and chocolate bars.

Gloriana stood as she approached. "Young lady, you are my hero." Eyeing the tray, she added, "What a beautiful presentation." She winked at Ky. "My mother has taught you well."

Her praise had Ky's smile growing even wider.

But Justin was no longer in the mood for s'mores or a campfire. Who did Gloriana think she was, calling him out on his faith? Though he was curious what she'd been about to say. Could it be that she'd lost someone she loved, too?

Chapter Seven

"That's right, Tucker, this year's Hope Crossing Fair and Rodeo is going to be one for the record books." Phone pressed to her ear, Gloriana paced her bedroom the following Friday morning as her interview with Tucker Ford, the morning show host at Houston's number one country music station, wound down. And thanks to a phone call from Landon Hightower last night, she had some breaking news. "Not only will Mandy Brinkman *and* Landon Hightower be signing autographs, we'll also have a *very* special guest performing at the Hope Crossing Dance Hall Saturday night."

"Rumor has it that guest is Luke Phillips," said Tucker. "Can you confirm that?"

"I sure can. Tickets go on sale May first." After all the locals had an opportunity to get theirs. "Folks can find more information on our website." She rattled off the address.

When the call ended a few minutes later, Gloriana let out a contented sigh. *Thank You, Lord.*

She had two more radio interviews scheduled for next week and a couple of remote television segments later in

April, for which she still needed to gather photos and put together a video montage. However, if they went as well as this one, the Hope Crossing Fair and Rodeo would live to see another year.

She grabbed her tablet from the white-painted dresser and made a note, because if they had the kind of turnout she was anticipating, there was no way the dance hall could hold everyone. They'd need to come up with a plan for overflow that included bleacher, tent and maybe even dance-floor rentals.

As she tapped her notes into the device, she found herself wishing she could talk things over with Justin. But given he'd barely spoken to her since that night around the campfire, except when he'd asked her to pass the ham during Easter dinner, it didn't seem likely. She hadn't meant for their conversation to grow so intense, though she couldn't say she regretted it, either. The fact that Justin had lost his wife was sad, but to lose his faith in God, as well—that was a crying shame.

Notes complete, she tossed the device on the queen-size bed topped with a frilly white comforter and shoved her feet into a pair of flip-flops before making her way downstairs at five till eight, dressed in her favorite yoga pants and a ratty Nashville T-shirt.

In the kitchen, Mom sat at the table, nursing a cup of coffee. It had been almost three weeks since her surgery, and while she still had to take things slow, the light had finally returned to her eyes.

"Good morning." Gloriana grabbed the plain white mug she'd left sitting beside the sink earlier.

"How'd the interview go?"

"Great." Taking hold of the coffeepot, she poured the dark roast, savoring its enticing aroma. "Once we were off the air, Tucker even said he'd like to bring his family out for the event. Give his kids a taste of country life." She retrieved the caramel-flavored creamer from the refrigerator and added a splash to her cup, watching it swirl through the steaming brew.

"Perhaps you should send him complimentary tickets."

Gloriana pulled out the chair beside her mother and sat down. "I was thinking the same thing." She blew across the top of her drink. "How are you feeling today?" While Mom was slowly but surely getting her strength back, the surgery had definitely messed with her schedule. Before, she would've had eggs collected and the island would be littered with fresh produce from the garden by now.

"Quite well, actually." Despite her smile, the creases in her brow told a different story.

"Why do you look worried, then?"

Mom waved her off. "I'm not worried. I just need to discuss something with you, that's all."

"Okay." Gloriana wrapped both hands around her mug, noting her short fingernails. With no nail salon in Hope Crossing and no time to go anywhere else, she'd decided to go *au naturel* for the first time in years. "What's up?"

Mom looked from Gloriana to her coffee cup and back again. "I've been mulling over Bill's marriage proposal."

Gloriana sucked in a sharp breath. "I see." She'd known this was coming, though she hadn't expected it quite so soon.

She shifted in her seat as happiness for her mother warred with a heaping helping of uncertainty. She was thrilled Mom had found love again, but she couldn't help wondering where that left her. After all, it was no secret that Bill didn't care for her. Even though he'd started speaking to her again, asking how her day went or if she needed help with anything around the house. Still, she couldn't help feeling as though he was merely tolerating her for the sake of her mother. Which had Gloriana wondering what things would be like once they were married.

"Glory?"

She looked at her mother.

"I know things were a little tense between you and Bill at the hospital."

A little? Like Harvey was a *little* hurricane?

"And don't think I haven't noticed how you make yourself scarce whenever he comes around." Mom sent her a knowing look. "I know you weren't to blame for what happened after my surgery, and Bill does, too. He's ashamed of how he treated you."

"Then why doesn't he apologize so we can move on down the road?"

"Because he'd have to make himself vulnerable, and you know how men are."

Recalling how her father always kept her at arm's length and the way Cody seemed to have no problem turning his back on her as soon as he found out she was pregnant, Gloriana shook her head. "No, I guess I don't know how they are, Mom."

"They don't go for all that touchy-feely stuff like we women do. They're afraid it'll make them look weak."

"Guess that's why they say it takes a big man to admit when he's wrong."

"I expect so." Mom lifted her cup. "Now I have a question for you."

Gloriana watched and waited.

"Are you comfortable with me accepting his proposal?"

She smiled. "Of course." Though she'd likely end up

feeling like an outsider once again. Like she was living on the fringes. Even when she was growing up, Hawkins was the one her folks had always leaned on. The one who'd worked alongside Daddy to help build Prescott Farms, whether it was working cattle, plowing fields or bringing in the pecan crop. The one who was Daddy's hunting buddy and got to stay with him at the cabin.

Gloriana had always envied their relationship. So much that she found herself doing a lot of stupid things to get Daddy's attention, never imagining they'd haunt her the rest of her life. Back then, though, she didn't care, because she'd had her sights set on leaving. If only she'd realized then that her Heavenly Father loved her unconditionally and longed to spend time with her.

Setting a hand atop her mother's, she said, "I want nothing more than for you to be happy."

Mom still looked hesitant. "If I were to say yes, would you be my maid of honor and help me plan the wedding?"

Despite her conflicted feelings about Bill, Gloriana found herself blinking back tears of joy. Her mother actually wanted her help. "I would be honored, Mom." She stood and moved to hug her mother, only to be interrupted by the doorbell.

As they parted, Mom said, "That'd be Bonnie Booker. She called and said she was dropping off a casserole."

Gloriana lifted her brow. "Does that mean I don't have to cook tonight?"

Mom nodded and started for the door. "It also means we'll be eating lasagna for the foreseeable future."

"Fine by me. I love lasagna." Gloriana grabbed the handled basket near the back door. "If you need me, I'll be gathering eggs." Not to mention sorting through her jumbled emotions.

Outside, the morning sun was warm on her skin. Dew dampened her toes as she moved into the yard, searching the countryside, hoping to see Justin. Her words had definitely struck a nerve with him. And just when they were starting to become friends. Now they were back to square one. Honestly, she kind of missed him.

Shaking off the unwanted thoughts, she continued toward the chicken coop. Maybe it was time for her to start looking for another job. After all, she knew her time in Hope Crossing was only temporary. Though she had to admit, leaving Prescott Farms didn't hold the appeal it once had. Visiting just wasn't the same as living here.

She had yet to mend any fences. But at the same time, she felt as though she was doing some good, helping revive the fair and rodeo, coaching Kyleigh… But was that enough to make her stay long term?

She opened the gate on the run surrounding the chicken coop and was promptly rushed by nearly a dozen hens. "Sorry, ladies. I'm running late today."

Meanwhile the rooster glared at her from the far corner.

"Are you coming out or what?" She didn't relish the idea of going in there until the creepy bird was out.

As if understanding, he cautiously strutted toward the opening, giving her a once-over before racing to freedom.

After collecting several eggs in a variety of colors, she continued to the garden to harvest some red lettuce for lunch. She was on her way out, closing the gate behind her, when she glimpsed that wretched bird again. And he didn't look happy.

A chill skittered up her spine as her gaze narrowed on the rooster. "What is your problem?"

Suddenly, he bolted toward her.

In her attempt to escape, she tripped. And while she managed to catch herself, a couple of eggs spilled from her basket and crashed to the ground.

Obviously taking advantage of the situation, the rooster took a flying leap toward her, crashing into her leg.

"Ow!"

Before she could regain her wits, he let out a screech and darted toward her again.

She ran, but he wasn't easily deterred.

"Get *away*—" She turned as he flew toward her again. That's when she saw that nasty clawlike spur sticking out of his leg. Right before he slammed into her again.

She shrieked as it penetrated her yoga pants. Moments later, blood seeped through the gray fabric, and her shin began to throb.

Her heart racing, she scanned the yard. When she didn't see the rooster anywhere, she made a break for the house.

Suddenly, something that sounded like mixture of screeching and crowing met her ears. Darting a glance over her shoulder, she saw enemy number one racing toward her at lightning speed.

Sweat beaded her brow as she moved right, then left, hoping to either lose him or wear him out. The ornery critter was too fast, though. He cut her off and took aim at her once again.

The eggs and lettuce went flying, and something akin to a scream spilled out of her as the dastardly bird nailed her other leg.

How was she going to get away from this crazy thing? No one else was around except her mother and Bonnie.

And not only was Mom in no shape to rescue Gloriana, they probably couldn't even hear her inside the house.

As the rooster regrouped, his beady eyes never leaving her, she tearfully lifted a prayer. *God, help me.*

She'd barely finished when he charged her once more. Turning, she slammed into something hard.

Justin?

He scooped her into his arms, all the while kicking at the rooster until he'd carried her through the side gate to safety.

She could feel his heart pounding wildly beneath her fingers, saw the determination etched in his tanned face.

With one arm still snugged around her waist, he set her feet on the ground beneath the shade of an oak tree.

"Thank you." Still trying to catch her breath, she lifted her gaze to find him staring at her, his chest rising and falling every bit as quickly as hers. And the intensity of his gaze stirred feelings Gloriana had promised herself she'd never feel again. She'd been rejected by both her father and her husband. She would not allow another man to do that ever again. So why couldn't she bring herself to look away?

Something flickered in Justin's gorgeous eyes, and, for a moment, she was lost in their depths. Then his brow knit a thousand different ways, right before he released her, hurried to his pickup and disappeared in a cloud of dust.

Justin barely eased his foot off the gas pedal until he reached the east pasture, where Bill waited with a couple of other ranchers and a hired hand who'd come to help work cattle. Justin wasn't sure what that jolt had been that shot through him the moment his eyes connected with

Gloriana's, but he knew beyond a shadow of a doubt that picking her up and holding her close had been a monumental mistake. One that messed with his head and stirred feelings he didn't want to feel. Not now, not ever.

He'd just emerged from the barn, where he'd been gathering vaccine supplies, when he'd heard her cry out. Like a fool, he went running off to check on her when he should have left well enough alone. After all, he'd been stewing on their campfire conversation for a week now, making sure he avoided her at all costs for fear she'd start in on him again.

He huffed out a breath as he closed in on the wooden pens where the four men waited on him. Best he could figure, the only reason he was so bent out of shape over this whole thing with Gloriana was because she was right. He was mad at God and had been throwing a tantrum for the last three years because he hadn't gotten his way. Barbie had died despite his pleas for God to spare her life.

Bill approached as Justin emerged from his truck into the morning sun. "I was wonderin' what happened to you."

Disgruntled cattle bellowed nearby, echoing Justin's mood as he glared at the older rancher. "I got interrupted, all right." The words came out harsher than he'd intended.

Bill considered him for a moment, his left eye twitching. "Coy and Reuben got the cattle penned—" he poked a thumb over his shoulder "—so we'd best not waste their time."

As the older man ambled away, Justin grabbed the cooler holding the vaccine and antibiotic bottles from the back seat, hating that his little stint as a hero had everyone waiting on him when he was supposed to be running the show.

"How's it going, Justin?" Jake Walker, a fellow rancher who also happened to be a widowed father like Justin, eyed him from beside the chute the cattle would be funneled into just long enough to receive their inoculations.

"It's going."

Bill nudged his hat back a notch as he watched the other two fellows separate the herd, allowing only heifers to pass into the chute first. "If I had to guess, I'd say someone got up on the wrong side of the bed this mornin'." He glanced back at Justin. "Everything all right?"

Justin couldn't stop the sarcastic laugh that puffed out. He hadn't been all right in a very long time, but things had gotten even worse this past week. All Gloriana's talk about how God loved her enough to pursue her even when she chose not to trust Him had embedded itself in Justin's brain. Ever since Barbie's death, he'd been pouting, wallowing in self-pity, trying to do everything— including raising Ky—in his own strength instead of taking his grievances to God. Worst of all, he realized what a hypocrite he'd become. Leaving it to the church to instill godly doctrines in his daughter, all the while turning his back on the same God he wanted her to know so she'd grow into a godly woman like her mother.

But there was no way he was going to admit that to Bill or anyone else.

After handing off repeater syringes and meds to Bill and Jake, Justin approached the chute with his own as the first heifer charged forward. "Just eager to get this finished."

Over the next hour and a half, they ran half a dozen heifers, two dozen cows, three bulls and fifteen calves through the chute. Now, Reuben and Coy had trailered their horses and were following Jake out of the pasture.

Bill watched as Justin loaded equipment back into his truck. "Whadda ya say we head up to Plowman's and grab a cup of coffee?"

"Not today."

"Looks like you've got a lot on your mind. Reckon you've got your hands full with the rodeo, huh?"

Justin nodded.

"Francie said Gloriana was s'posed to have a radio interview this morning. S'pose I'll stop in to say hi and see how it went."

Justin faced the older rancher. "We still working at your place next week?" Just like today, the other fellows would help out.

The older man nodded. "Wednesday mornin'."

Reaching for the door handle on his truck, Justin forced a smile. "I'll be there with bells on." Or at least in a better mood. He hoped.

While Bill headed to Francie's, Justin went back to his cabin for an early lunch. Not that he was all that hungry. But maybe a tall drink of ice water would improve his mood. Though it was still early April, that sun was a scorcher today. Hopefully it wasn't a sign of things to come.

He parked in front of the cabin and went inside. After filling a large cup with ice, he went to the sink and turned on the water, noting the breakfast dishes he and Ky had left behind in their mad dash to get out the door this morning. So, after a couple of gulps, he set the cup aside and opened the dishwasher.

Unfortunately, the mundane task left his mind free to wander into territory Justin would just as soon avoid.

Barbie would be beyond upset with him for turning his back on God. They'd prayed for years that He would bring them a child, then had stood before their church, promising to pray for Ky and bring her up in the instruction of the Lord. Now, it nearly wrecked him to think how he'd dropped the ball. When was the last time he'd even prayed for Ky?

He'd just settled the last bowl into the rack when there was a knock at the door. "Who could that be?" Not that it mattered. Actually, he ought to thank whoever it was for saving him from his thoughts.

Grabbing a dish towel, he wiped his hands and tossed it on the counter before moving to the door. When he opened it, irritation mingled with an unwanted thrill. "Gloriana?" She'd changed clothes and was now wearing a stylish T-shirt with a pair of skinny jeans and flip-flops, and her silky hair was pulled back into a ponytail.

His gaze drifted to the plate in her hand. Were those chocolate chip cookies beneath that plastic wrap?

"I was hoping you'd still be here." She drew in a seemingly nervous breath. "I wanted to thank you again for helping me get away from that rooster." She gestured to the cookies.

When he hesitated a little too long, she added, "Can we talk? I realize things have been a little tense between us, but I wanted to update you on the ad campaign."

That he could talk about. So long as the conversation didn't stray the way it had that night around the fire.

"I've a got a few minutes." He stepped aside, allowing her to enter, and for the second time today, his thoughts betrayed him as the aroma of honeysuckle enveloped him. "How's the leg?" He'd seen traces of blood on her pants. "That rooster didn't get you too bad, did he?"

"Thankfully, the damage was superficial." She paused beside the peninsula that separated the kitchen from the living space and set the plate on the butcher-block counter. "Help yourself. They were made fresh this morning."

Closing the door, he moved toward her. "I do love your mama's chocolate chip cookies."

"Don't we all. I made these, though."

He looked at her as she peeled back the plastic wrap, recalling the Easter meal she'd prepared. It had been every bit as delicious as Francie's meals. "It's a risk I'm willing to take."

The pink that crept into her cheeks did strange things to his psyche.

Turning away, he said, "What did you want to talk about?" He took a bite. This definitely wasn't her mother's cookie. Something was different. He didn't think it was possible, but it tasted even better than Francie's version.

"So, I did a segment on the rodeo with one of the country stations out of Houston this morning."

"I heard it."

"You—you did?"

Facing her, he nodded. "I was taking Ky to school. She insisted we listen."

"Oh." Her hazel eyes drifted to the wood floor.

Why did she look so disappointed? And why did that bother him?

"Well, I checked the numbers on the rodeo website both before and after the interview, and in the hour after the interview, we had over five hundred hits."

He nearly choked on the last of his cookie. "Five hundred?"

"I know, I was shocked, too."

Reaching for his drink, he said, "That's more than last year's total attendance." He took a sip as she nodded.

"And that was just *one* market. Which means we need to come up with a plan to accommodate all those extra people who'll be attending. I'm not so worried about the rodeo. However, the dance hall can only hold so many."

"Yeah, I guess you're right." He moved around the peninsula.

"But, before we get into what's bound to be a lengthy discussion, I want to apologize for coming down on you so hard last week. I should have exercised a little more compassion instead of stirring up a hornet's nest."

He turned to find her standing behind him, looking remorseful. Not to mention, way too pretty.

Drawing in a hefty breath that was laced with honeysuckle, he said, "As much as I hate to admit it, your little tongue-lashing was probably the wake-up call I needed, because I've been thinking about it ever since."

She bit her bottom lip as if trying to hide a smile. "I'm sorry."

"Don't be. You forced me to take a long, hard look at myself. And I didn't particularly like what I saw. I've deprived my daughter of the kind of father she deserves. One who leads by example, instead of expecting others to pick up the slack."

"Don't be so hard on yourself. You're a good father."

He lifted a shoulder. "Maybe, but what Ky needs most is a godly father."

Gloriana nodded, her smile sorrowful. "So what are you going to do?"

Scratching his head, he said, "Considering I just now took the first step in admitting how wrong I've been, I have no clue. But I know where to go to find the answers." He patted his Bible that sat atop the counter, collecting dust except for a couple hours on Sundays.

She smiled in earnest then. "Sounds like a great place to start."

He peered down at her, his thoughts again drifting back to that night around the fire when he'd asked her if she'd ever lost someone she loved. She'd started to answer, but Ky had interrupted. And he'd been curious ever since. Had Gloriana lost someone she loved? And did he dare bring it up now?

Before he could come up with an opening, though, she moved to the opposite side of the counter and reached for a cookie. "So, what do we do about the dance hall?"

Chapter Eight

Despite the board's scheduled workday to clean up the fairgrounds this coming Saturday, Gloriana decided to scope things out for herself Monday morning and bring her memory up to speed. Not only did time have a way of distorting one's perspective, things could've changed in the past sixteen years, and she didn't want to be surprised. And now that Mom was a full three weeks post op, Gloriana felt more comfortable leaving her on occasion. Especially after seeing how well her mother had done at church yesterday. Being around all those people for the first time in weeks had really energized her.

A lively Christian song belted from the radio as Gloriana continued along the farm to market road, savoring the unobstructed view. Then her phone cut in and her agent's name appeared on the vehicle's touch screen. They hadn't spoken since the day Gloriana notified her she'd resigned, so Marlena was probably growing concerned. Or simply curious.

Gloriana pressed the button on her steering wheel. "Good morning, Marlena."

"Good morning to you. How are things in Texas? How is your mother?"

Gloriana gave her a quick rundown of everything that had gone on in the past few weeks. Eyeing the fairgrounds' entrance ahead, she turned on her blinker and eased onto the shoulder. "And just so you'll know, once Mom is well enough for me to start thinking about going back to work, I want to limit my search to Texas. Dallas–Fort Worth, Houston, Austin, San Antonio."

There was a lengthy pause. "That's rather constraining, don't you think? Not to mention, the Austin and San Antonio markets are smaller than what you're used to."

"I'm aware." Gloriana turned into the gravel drive, continuing past the dance hall and across the parking lot to the fairgrounds. "But I want to be closer to my family."

Marlena's silence stretched on longer than usual. No doubt stunned by Gloriana's about-face. Until recently, she'd only been interested in rising to the top, no matter where it took her.

Finally, "I will keep my eyes and ears open, then."

They exchanged goodbyes as Gloriana parked near the main gate. She got out, donning her sunglasses to survey the sixty-some acres that were home to an outdoor rodeo arena, livestock and entertainment pavilions, and an exhibit barn. And while the place looked rather forlorn, in her mind's eye she could see the field bustling with fairgoers, hear the playful sounds of the midway and the booming voice of the rodeo announcer while the aromas of smoked meat, popcorn and cotton candy wafted through the warm June air.

Determined to return the event to its former glory, she strolled the grounds through shin-high grass, grateful she'd worn jeans and boots, looking to see if anything had changed.

After reminiscing at the arena, she moved on to the entertainment pavilion, where bands would play while fairgoers escaped the sun as they sampled smoked meats from the barbecue cook-off that took place under a nearby canopy of oak trees. How sad that the cook-off had dropped Hope Crossing from its circuit. She would not let the rodeo meet the same fate.

Turning, she lifted her gaze, her heart sinking when she caught sight of the back of the exhibit hall. Vandals had spray-painted the building. And very poorly, at that. The haphazard streaks of black and red that stretched across the beige metal surface weren't even worthy of being called graffiti. Though the damage remained the same.

Moving closer, she spotted several spray-paint cans littering the grass. She picked one up as the sound of tires on gravel signaled someone in the parking lot. Hoping it wasn't the perpetrators coming back to do more damage, she peeked around the building, only to see a sheriff's SUV.

Her gut tightened when Brady emerged from the vehicle. After the way he'd dismissed her at the board meeting, she wasn't sure what to expect.

Lord, give me the words to say. Please, I want Brady to know that I've changed and that I'm sincerely sorry for the pain I caused him.

She could tell the moment he spotted her. His expression turned grim as he continued toward her, his gaze moving to the can she held right before he rounded the building and surveyed the damage.

"I suppose you're going to tell me you had nothing

to do with this." His accusatory glance let her know he wasn't interested in listening to anything she had to say.

She huffed out an indignant snort. "No, I did not. But I'm going to fix it." With that, she thrust the can into his hand and marched to her SUV, unwilling to let anyone or anything ruin this year's fair.

As she peeled out of the parking lot and made her way to the main road, she glanced at the dance hall, then did a quick a double take. It, too, bore the scars of the same abuse the exhibit hall had suffered. Black and red paint spelled out filthy words. And with the white paint already peeling from the wooden boards, nothing short of a paint job would remedy that situation.

After checking in with her mother and learning that one of her friends from church had dropped by for lunch, Gloriana headed straight to Plowman's, where, wonder of all wonders, she found some graffiti remover, saving her a trip to the big box store in Brenham. After loading every bottle they had into her cart, she grabbed some rags, steel wool and a five-gallon bucket and headed for the checkout counter.

On her way back to the fairgrounds she was haunted by the suspicious look in Brady's blue eyes. And while she couldn't say she blamed him, surely they had security cameras around the fairgrounds to aid in catching the perpetrators. Just like they'd had at the ag barn back in high school. Of course, she hadn't been aware of those until she learned Brady had been expelled from school.

A deep sorrow washed over her as she recalled how self-absorbed she'd been back then, thinking of no one but herself and nothing but getting out of Hope Crossing. So when she hadn't been able to talk the ag teacher into giving her a retest on the exam she'd failed, thus bringing her grade average down and threatening her opportunity of getting into Texas Tech, she'd wanted revenge.

Aware that Brady, a quiet kid who was a year younger and a bit of a loner, had a crush on her, she'd talked him into helping her release the animals from the school's ag barn, foolishly believing their teacher would be the one in trouble for not making sure things were secure.

Imagine her surprise when she got to school the next day and everyone was saying that Brady had been arrested by his dad, the sheriff, after the school's new security camera got a shot of the license plate on Brady's old pickup. The story wasn't completely true. Brady had not been arrested, only expelled. However, his father sent him away to a military school for his senior year. And through it all, Gloriana's name never came up. Brady took his licks without ever fingering her, while she'd remained silent.

Shrugging off the self-loathing that accompanied the memory, she pulled into the once again empty fairgrounds. The heat had her ditching her button-down shirt in favor of the tank top she wore beneath it. Then she pulled her hair back into a ponytail, located a spigot, filled the bucket and set to work on the exhibit barn.

It didn't take her long to figure out this was a much bigger job than she'd anticipated. She'd thought the remover would take the graffiti right off the way acetone removed nail polish, yet as she swapped her rag for some steel wool, she realized this wasn't going to be so easy. She would keep trying, though.

With a mix of contemporary Christian and country songs echoing from her phone in the back pocket of her jeans, she focused on the task at hand. Then nearly jumped out of her skin when Brady sneaked around the corner of the building an hour later.

"What *are* you doing?"

After regaining her wits, she resumed scrubbing the metal surface. "Isn't it rather obvious?"

"Yes, but why?"

Frustrated, she paused, swiping the back of her hand across her brow before sweat dripped into her eyes. "Because I owe it to the town. I am *not* the same Gloriana Prescott you and everyone else remembers, and I wish folks would just get over it and move on." She finally met his gaze. "Including you. I know what I did was beyond wrong, and I've been trying to apologize, but you won't even give me the opportunity. I feel horrible for what I did to you. And if I could go back and undo everything, I would. But I can't. All I can do is say I'm sorry. And now that I've done that, I need to get back to work."

Though she continued scrubbing, she could still see Brady out of the corner of her eye. He seemed to be contemplating her outburst. Until his radio crackled to life. Gloriana listened as the female dispatcher relayed information about an automobile accident north of town.

Pressing a button, he spoke into the mic on his collar. "I'm on my way." He stared at her for a long moment, and she wondered—hoped—he might accept her apology, as rushed and self-pitying as it had been. Instead, he walked away without a word.

She returned to her work, trying to ignore the disappointment prodding her heart. At least she'd finally gotten to say her piece. What happened now was in God's hands.

As the sun's heat intensified and her muscles began to ache, she stepped back to check her progress. Tears pricked her eyes when she realized she hadn't tackled but a quarter of the surface.

The sound of tires on gravel again echoed from the parking lot. Yet while she expected to see Brady rounding the corner, it was Bill.

Just what she didn't need. One more person believing the graffiti was her doing.

He tipped his straw hat back, his gaze going from the building to her. "Looks like you could use some help."

Her mother must have told him what she was doing and insisted he help her. "Probably, but you've got your own work to do."

"Nothing that can't wait." He glanced from her to the parking lot. "I'll be right back."

Between the heat and her frustratingly slow progress, Gloriana's mood was quickly shifting into the foul category, so the last person she wanted helping her was Bill.

When he reappeared, he was pulling a power washer with one hand and holding a bottle of water in the other. And judging by the condensation dripping off said bottle, it was cold.

"Here." He shoved the bottle toward her. "You look like you could use this." Was he actually smiling?

"Thank you." She took hold of the bottle, twisted off the lid and took a long swig, the cool water soothing her parched throat. "What's with the power washer?"

"Well, I'm hoping it'll make quick work of removing this poor attempt at artwork." He pointed to the wall.

Eyeing him suspiciously, she said, "Did my mother put you up to this?"

"No, ma'am. I ran into Brady. He was out by my place, taking a report on an accident. He mentioned he'd run into you and what you were doing. Thought I'd see if I could make things easier for you."

"Why would you want to do that?" After all, he hadn't been around much lately. Mom had suggested it was because he was busy working cattle, which meant she had yet to tell him she was ready to accept his proposal. Still, Gloriana couldn't help wondering if his absence had more to do with avoiding her.

Hands on his Wrangler-covered hips, he glanced from her to the ground before slowly returning. "Figure it's the least I can do after the way I treated you at the hospital."

She replaced the cap on her bottle in stunned silence.

"To make matters worse, I've let things fester ever since. I'm sorry, Gloriana. You weren't responsible for Francie's fall, and I knew it then just as well as I know the back of my hand. But I was…scared." His shoulders slumped as he lowered his head.

Gloriana wasn't sure she'd ever been more taken aback. He wasn't here because of Mom's intervention; he genuinely wanted to help—and relieve himself of the burden that had plagued him for weeks. Gloriana could relate to that all too well.

"Because you love her. And you were afraid of losing her."

He looked at her again, his eyes misty. "I surely was."

"You weren't entirely wrong, though. I shouldn't have left her."

"You needed to talk to your brother. No one would've imaged she'd try to get out of bed."

"You're right about that." Gloriana still couldn't wrap her head around it.

Bill cleared his throat. "I know I've been skeptical since the day you arrived, but over these past few weeks

I've seen what a fine young woman you've become, Gloriana. Your mama's been blessed to have you here. And I hope you can find it in your heart to forgive me."

As she studied the pained expression on the older man's face, knowing that only a few months ago she would've lashed back at him, she knew what she had to do. God had extended her more grace than she ever deserved. Who was she not to do the same for Bill?

"You're forgiven." Yet as grateful as she was to Bill for extending the proverbial olive branch, she found herself wishing other people in town could find it in their hearts to do the same for her.

While Ky joined Francie at her place Saturday morning, in part to do some baking—but also so the woman wouldn't be alone all day—Justin stood in the parking lot at the fairgrounds with at least seventy-five Hope Crossing residents who'd gathered under a cloudless sky for the annual spruce-up day. An event he'd always tried to get out of in the past. But then, Gloriana hadn't been there before.

Ever since that day she'd come by with the cookies, he'd found himself increasingly intrigued. She wasn't at all like the Gloriana he'd heard stories about during his time at Prescott Farms. Though she was still a spitfire, unafraid to go toe-to-toe with him or stand in front of a group of people who didn't have a whole lot of respect for her and convince them to accept her help.

Even Bill seemed to have softened toward her, lending help when she'd taken on the task of removing graffiti from the exhibit barn. And while Justin wondered if, perhaps, Francie hadn't had something to do with that, word around town was that Gloriana had been ready to tackle the job with or without assistance.

Now, having seen her very little this week, save for the one afternoon she'd worked with Ky and supper at Francie's another evening, Justin found himself scanning the crowd, hoping for an opportunity to visit with her. She was working with his daughter, after all, so it only made sense he'd want to get to know her a little better.

Nice try, buddy.

"All right, folks." Charlene stood in the bed of a pickup, wearing a pair of cutoff overalls and holding a megaphone as she addressed the group. "We've got a lot of work ahead of us today. In addition to the usual tasks of repairing pens and fences, mowing and general cleanup of both the grounds and the buildings, vandals have forced us to paint the exterior of our beloved dance hall."

A round of boos echoed from the crowd while others gave a thumbs-down to show their displeasure over the damage.

"Plowman's has graciously provided all of the paint and supplies," Charlene continued, "and several of our fine fellows have already scraped, sanded, caulked and primed the building, so now we just need some willing volunteers to paint."

More than a dozen hands went up, one of them attached to a beautiful woman with a silky, dark brown ponytail spilling out the back of her baseball cap.

Justin's hand joined the others as a strange sensation settled into his chest. For now, he'd chalk it up to the sausage biscuit he'd had for breakfast. Though he wished he'd held off until he got here. Countless people had brought in snacks, sandwiches and a bounty of baked goods that had his mouth watering.

Charlene dismissed everyone a short time later after encouraging them to fortify themselves with muffins, kolaches and pigs in a blanket.

Justin didn't need to be told twice. He headed straight for the kolaches, only to find Gloriana staring at them, looking cute in a pair of cutoff jeans and a Nashville T-shirt that had seen better days.

Moving beside her, he said, "Problem?"

"Yeah, these peach kolaches are calling my name."

"How is that a problem?"

"If I eat a whole one, I'll be too bloated to work." She stared longingly at the quickly disappearing pastries topped with assorted fruits.

"We could split one."

"Good idea. Thank you." She scooped one up and carefully pulled it apart before handing him his half. "There you go." A look of satisfaction played across her face as she took her first taste. "This is *so* good."

He'd just taken a bite when his phone rang in the breast pocket of his work shirt. "That's the Ky line. I hope everything's okay with your mother." He fished the phone out and answered. "Everything all right, Ky?"

"Yeah. But Callie asked if I could spend the night with her. Can I? I'll still be at church tomorrow."

Without Ky, he'd be facing a quiet evening alone. And those were always fraught with haunting memories. But that was his problem, not his daughter's. "Sure. I can run you over to their place after supper."

"But they're having pizza. *Real* pizza. Not the frozen kind we always have."

"Hey, I happen to like that freezer-burn flavor."

"Dad…"

"Okay, I'll take you before supper."

"Thank you, Daddy. I gotta go. Mrs. Francie and I are making brownies."

"Good, save me some."

Gloriana looked at him as he returned the phone to his pocket. "Let me guess. She's been invited to a sleepover?"

"How did you know?"

She lifted a shoulder. "I was once a teenager, too. And it's a Saturday." Inclining her head slightly, she said, "So what's the *Ky line*?"

"I carry two phones. The only people with the number for the Ky line are Ky, her grandparents and the school. Everyone else is relegated to the open line."

"Open line, huh?"

Thoughts of that day Barbie died prodded at his mind, but he shook them away. "Call me overprotective, but I just want to be sure my daughter is able to access me whenever needed."

The corners of Gloriana's mouth tipped upward. "Actually, I think that's very sweet. You're a good dad."

"I try."

"So what are you slated to work on today?"

Acting as though he had no idea what she was doing, he said, "Painting the dance hall."

Her eyes widened. "Me, too. Maybe we could work together." She seemed to catch herself, her smile evaporating. "That is, unless you'd prefer to work alone. Painting is a kind of a solitary thing, after all."

"True, but having someone to talk to makes the time pass much faster." Her bashful grin had him nodding toward the dance hall. "C'mon, let's go claim a spot."

They crossed the parking lot to the clapboard building that sat on a pier-and-beam foundation and sported a high-pitched tin roof to allow for ventilation before gently sloping over the two sides that appeared to have been added to the original structure. The top-hinged sheets of wood that normally covered the windowless openings along all three sides had been raised, held in place with wooden arms, allowing air to flow through. Something those who were working inside the building were sure to appreciate.

After collecting their paint and supplies, they went to work on the north side of the building, where a sprawling live oak afforded plenty of shade. With the aid of a ladder, Justin took the top section while Gloriana worked on the lower half.

"I've always loved this old dance hall." Her voice held an air of wonder. "You know, when Clay bought the property, he was only interested in the land. The rodeo arena was the main focus of his universe. A couple years later, one of the ag teachers suggested they add a livestock show." She dipped her brush into the paint can at her feet. "As the event grew in popularity, his wife recommended they turn it into a real country fair with a carnival, baking and canning competitions, and entertainment." After removing the excess paint, she again moved the brush across the wood in smooth strokes. "Then they fixed up the dance hall for a Saturday night dance, and it's been that way ever since. Well, until recent history, anyway."

"Yeah, bingo doesn't hold the same appeal as a dance." He climbed down off the ladder. "My guess is the board no longer had the funds to bring in a band."

Gloriana straightened to face him. "That's all the more reason they should fix up the dance hall."

A welcoming breeze rustled the leaves overhead.

"How do you figure?"

"Clay left the fairgrounds to the fair and rodeo board.

That means they own the dance hall. Why not rent it out for parties and wedding receptions? Sure, there would be a little cost up front to make it compliant, but do you have any idea how much these rustic venues rent for? They could have a nice stream of income." She puffed out a breath. "With Charlene being in real estate, I'm surprised she hasn't thought of that."

"You make a good point." He grabbed a water bottle and twisted off the cap. "There's just one problem."

"Which is?" She watched him.

"Someone would have to be willing to take ownership of a project like that. To oversee things on a regular basis. Take care of the rentals."

She smiled. "Sounds like a great job to me."

"Then, perhaps, you should do it."

"I think it would be fun." She stooped to dip her paintbrush again. "But, with Mom and Bill getting married, I'm afraid my time in Hope Crossing is limited." She started to paint, then paused. "You do know about my mother and Bill, right?"

Justin returned to the ladder, feeling more than a little off-kilter. "Yeah, but that doesn't mean you have to leave. What about Ky's lessons?"

"Don't worry, I'll be here through the rodeo. And Mom's decided on the last Saturday in May for her wedding." She sighed. "I also have to find another job, though I have to admit I'm kind of enjoying doing all of this promotion. It's challenged me and forced me to be more creative."

Justin understood all that. What he couldn't wrap his head around was why the thought of Gloriana leaving made him so incredibly sad. And why he felt the need to stop her.

"So, uh, is Bill going to be hanging out with Francie tonight?"

"Oh, I'm certain of it. Now that she's agreed to marry him, he comes around even more than before."

"In that case, could I interest you in an evening ride around the ranch?"

Under the brim of her ball cap, one pretty brow arched. "Depends. Are we talking UTV ride or horses?"

"Horses. Things are looking mighty pretty over at Hideaway Cove these days." Nestled at the far western edge of Prescott Farms, the five-acre tank brimming with bass was hidden among a dense growth of oaks, cedars and loblolly pines. "Have you been by there since you've been back?"

"I have not."

"Well, then, it sounds like you're due for a visit."

"That does sound nice. I could pack a picnic supper, if you'd like, and we could eat up there."

He nodded. "Now you're talkin'. The country version of dinner and a movie."

"Exactly."

"All right, then." While apprehension warred with excitement in his gut, he couldn't seem to contain his smile. "We'd best get this painting knocked out."

Chapter Nine

Gloriana stood in her mother's kitchen, her hands shaking as she struggled to tuck the contents of the picnic supper she'd prepared into the insulated saddlebags. Why was she so nervous? It wasn't like Justin had asked her on a date. He'd simply suggested an evening ride.

And then she'd been the one to take things a step further by adding supper to the mix.

Her entire being cringed. What was she thinking?

That you enjoyed his company and wouldn't mind getting to know him better.

As if that was supposed to make her feel better. She'd rarely dated since her divorce. When she did, it was only on the rare occasion when she was expected to have a date. Things like parties or charity events. Not just because.

I thought this wasn't a date.

A groan escaped her lips. This would be so much easier if she and Justin were still at odds with one another. Of course, then they wouldn't be going at all, and she was looking forward to seeing Hideaway Cove. She hadn't been there since right after her high school graduation. Tori had just gotten engaged. The two of them had spent the afternoon swimming and munching on pimento cheese sandwiches and Mom's chocolate chip cookies, all the while sharing their secret hopes and dreams.

Justin didn't strike her as the kind of guy who would be satisfied with a simple sandwich, though. So, after scouring the refrigerator, Gloriana shredded some left-over roast beef and piled it high on a couple of po' boy rolls, then topped the meat with pepper jack cheese and pepperoncini slices. Some baby carrots, red-pepper hummus and the brownies Mom and Kyleigh had made rounded out the meal, along with a couple of bottled waters. As she was about to head out the door, though, she found herself second-guessing the hummus and added some chips to the mix in case Justin wasn't a fan.

With the saddlebag draped over her shoulder, she said goodbye to Mom and Bill and exited the house a little before six fifteen. She'd showered as soon as she got home from painting at the dance hall, then stressed over what to wear, not wanting to appear as though she was trying too hard. After asking herself what she'd wear if it was Tori she was going riding with, she opted for a red-and-white-plaid shirt over a white tank top, faded jeans, and the old Ariats she'd only recently begun to consider replacing.

The evening air had cooled slightly, a refreshing change from earlier this afternoon and perfect for a ride. She and Justin had agreed to meet at the barn, yet as she rounded the side of the house, she spotted him coming up the drive atop Chester, his buckskin gelding, while holding Shadow's reins as she moseyed alongside them, head bobbing.

Gloriana settled a hand over her racing heart. Did that man look fine in the saddle or what? He'd traded his paint clothes for a pair of medium-wash jeans and a black T-shirt that further emphasized his muscular biceps. Throw in the fact that he'd chivalrously tacked up her ride and brought her to her, and her insides were doing backflips. Or perhaps it was the smile on his face that seemed to say he was looking forward to their time together.

"Evenin', ma'am." He touched the brim of his straw hat. "Looks like a mighty fine night for a ride."

"Indeed" was all she could manage to eke out without sounding like a love-struck teenager.

"I dropped Ky off a little early so I could meet you here. You know, like a proper date."

Date? Have mercy. If her heart beat any faster, she might pass out.

Praying he wouldn't see the heat in her cheeks, she focused on securing her saddlebags. "That was very sweet. Thank you."

With a deep breath, she mounted Shadow, relaxing as they headed down the drive, winding their way past the cabin, along the edge of the woods and into the pasture, all the while discussing today's events, how they'd managed to complete the painting of the dance hall, and the ripening dewberries they spotted in the thickets along the way.

"I'll have to come out next week to do some picking," Gloriana commented as they wound around a live oak motte.

"Ky loves dewberries," Justin said from behind her. "Your mom has really instilled that living-off-the-land attitude in her."

"Perhaps she'd like to join me, then. That is, if you

don't mind." Her body swayed as she peered over her shoulder to see Justin rubbing the back of his neck.

"Yeah... This would probably be a good time for me to admit I misjudged you." He caught up to her as they approached the entrance to Hideaway Cove. "You were right when you said I had a preconceived notion of you based on hearsay. That was my mistake. Because the Gloriana I've gotten to know is anything but self-serving and is trying hard to make amends."

She swallowed the sudden lump in her throat. First Bill, now Justin. *God, thank You.*

Daring to meet his gaze, she said, "I appreciate you saying that, Justin. More than you know."

A simple nod was his only response.

Eager to lighten the mood, she urged Shadow onto the narrow trail, ducking beneath a pine bough. A few minutes later, they emerged from the trees to the place that had once been her escape from the world. Taking in the glassy lake enveloped by trees, Gloriana breathed deep, the scent of pine filling her senses. And, oddly enough, making her feel as though she was home.

Moving to a grassy area a short distance away, near a pier that jutted over the water, they dismounted, allowing the horses to graze.

"I brought a blanket." Justin removed it from the back of his saddle while she retrieved their meal.

"Good thinking. That completely slipped my mind." She watched as he spread out the worn quilt.

"Consider it my contribution to our dining experience." He settled onto one side, drawing his knees up as he removed his cowboy hat. "Speaking of dining—" he watched her open the insulated bag "—I'm starving."

"Me, too."

She laid out the food, surprised when he said, "I love hummus."

"You're kidding." She swiped her hair behind her ears.

"Okay, I'll admit I was skeptical the first time Barbie made me try it, but it's actually good."

Gloriana arched a brow. "Then perhaps you should give Brussels sprouts another try."

He shook his head. "Nope. Not happening."

Laughing, she handed him a sandwich. "Hopefully this will meet with your approval."

She gathered her own sandwich and peeled back the foil as he took his first bite.

"Mmm." He stared at the sandwich until he finished chewing. "This is delicious. Definitely not the average roast beef sandwich."

His appreciation had her smiling. "The pepperoncini gives it a nice zing."

"I never would've thought of that. This is way better than the boring roast beef with mayo I usually make."

Hunger had them focusing on their food for the next several minutes instead of conversation.

"That hit the spot." He wadded up his foil and reached for more carrots.

"I'm glad you liked it." Her sandwich gone, she handed him a plastic-wrapped brownie and grabbed one for herself. "I'm curious, how did you end up at Prescott Farms?"

"After Barbie died, I was ready to escape the city and get back to my roots." He unwrapped his dessert. "I'd always wanted to be a ranch manager like my dad. He put the word out to his rancher friends that I was lookin', and someone along the way mentioned Prescott Farms. So I contacted your brother, and after a long talk, he asked me to come down to meet with him, your mother and Carl."

Carl was the oft-grumpy cowboy who'd run the ranch prior to Justin.

"Hope Crossing is a long way from your family in north Texas." She picked off a piece of brownie and popped it in her mouth.

"It is. But something just felt right about this place. And neither your mom nor Hawkins was put off by the fact that I was a single dad." He smiled. "On the contrary, your mother was tickled to death. She embraced Ky as if she was her own granddaughter from the day we arrived."

"With Hawkins and me both gone, having you and Kyleigh here filled a void in my mother's life." And for that, Gloriana was grateful.

"She's a pretty special lady, all right." He paused, staring at her. "Please don't be upset with me for asking this, but why didn't you come home more often?"

Embarrassed, Gloriana wadded up the now-empty plastic wrap, shrugging. "I was too busy building my career."

He leaned toward her, nudging her shoulder with his own. "One should never be too busy for family."

Looking at him, she said, "I know that now."

Glancing at the lake, Justin did a double take before touching a finger to his lips and leaning closer. Close enough that she could smell the woody scent of his soap. "Look across the lake." The whispered words tickled her cheek, sending a shiver down her spine.

She had to force herself to focus. When she did, she spotted a doe with her fawn. Something that wasn't an uncommon occurrence at the ranch. However— "I've never seen one so tiny," she whispered. Its little legs trembled, and its movements were awkward.

"It can't be more than a day old," he said.

The mama's head jerked in their direction. She must've heard them.

Gloriana held her breath, and only in part because of the deer. Justin was so close she could feel the warmth radiating from him.

The doe stomped her front leg. A split second later, she snorted before she and her baby disappeared into the woods.

"That was incredible." Gloriana turned only to discover Justin's face mere inches from hers.

"Yeah, it was." He stood, and she found herself missing his nearness. Then he held out a hand. "Let's walk."

Unfortunately, he released his hold once she was on her feet.

The conversation transitioned to the mundane as they moved to the water's edge—Kyleigh, barrel racing and more talk about today.

Justin picked up a rock and skipped it across the surface of the water. "There's something I've been curious about since that night around the campfire."

She relaxed, knowing she'd been completely up front with him that night, about who she was and where she stood regarding her faith. "Which is?"

"When I spitefully asked if you've ever been robbed of someone you loved, your partial response, before Ky interrupted, left me wondering." He faced her. "Have you lost someone?"

Gloriana suddenly found herself looking at the treetops, the ripples on the water and everywhere except at Justin. She'd made that comment in the heat of the moment, reacting to his excuse for not trusting God. But would she really have told him about her daughter?

Those long months, alone and pregnant, had been the most heartbreaking of her life. And if it hadn't been for the child growing inside her, she wasn't sure she would have survived. But she'd refused to let her baby down, because he or she was counting on Gloriana more than anyone ever had. She ate right, took her vitamins, willed herself to get enough sleep and put one foot in front of the other each and every day. Then she'd blessed some happy couple with a child they'd, no doubt, longed for.

Until now, Tori was the only person who knew Gloriana's secret. And she planned to keep it that way. Still, that hadn't been her only loss.

When her gaze finally met Justin's, she inhaled deeply. "I was married briefly. Back in college." She lifted a shoulder, recalling how badly she wanted to be loved and how painful Cody's rejection had been. "Shortly after the end of our freshman year, we ran off to Las Vegas and got married. Four months later, he walked out on us, claiming that marrying me had been the biggest mistake of his life." And while it wasn't the first time she'd felt as though she'd been a mistake, it had solidified her resolve to never grant another man the power to hurt her again.

"Us?"

She looked up to find Justin's confused gaze fixed on her. "What?"

"You said, 'He walked out on *us*.'"

She felt her eyes widen as her brain scrambled to keep up. Talk about a Freudian slip. "Oh. I—just meant us, as in him and me. A couple. You know."

Justin nodded, the lines in his brow deepening as he reached for her. "I'm sorry you had to go through that."

He squeezed her hand. "That guy obviously didn't have a clue what real love was all about." His gaze never leaving hers, he continued, "I guess you do understand where I was coming from."

She nodded, her mouth suddenly dry.

"Thank you for sharing that with me." The look in his blue-green eyes stirred something inside her. A longing for more than just a career and respect. She wanted the impossible—the kind of relationship her mom and dad had. That Justin and Barbie had. To love and be loved so deeply that it erased all doubt. Something so intimate that you knew what the other person was thinking before they even said it.

But that meant she'd have to open the heart she'd kept closed tighter than a steel drum. And that was something only God could do.

She glanced at the suddenly darkening sky. "We should head back."

Late Tuesday afternoon, Justin sat behind the wheel of the UTV, grateful Gloriana and Ky had already planned to do some dewberry picking after school. When Gloriana had proposed the idea over Sunday dinner at Francie's, he'd figured it'd give him an opportunity to head to Brenham for a pantry-stocking grocery run. Instead, he found himself traversing every inch of Prescott Farms' two thousand acres in search of a wayward cow that was ready to calve. And while it wasn't uncommon for cows to slip away when they were about to give birth, he'd thought he knew all their hiding places. Obviously, he was wrong.

His frustration mounted as he combed pastures, woods and thickets, and due only in part to the missing cow.

The rest could only be attributed to what seemed to be a severe case of Gloriana on the brain. Especially as he scoured the area around Hideaway Cove.

Not only was the woman beautiful, she was compassionate, determined and comfortable in her own skin. She made him feel alive again, and he was drawn to her like a moth to light. Kind of ironic for a guy who vowed he'd never even date again. Was his attitude changing?

Pausing at the spot where they'd picnicked, he peered over the water, recalling the pain in Gloriana's eyes when she'd told him about her ex. Justin didn't care how tough Gloriana might appear to be, her ex's words must have felt like a knife to the heart. Why had the guy married her in the first place? Did he not stop to consider they were called vows for a reason?

Justin shook his head, wondering what was worse, having one's spouse snatched away unexpectedly by death or watching them walk away for purely selfish reasons. Though the more he thought about it, the clearer it became that there wasn't a whole lot of difference. Gloriana hadn't been able to stop her husband from leaving any more than Justin had been able to stop Barbie from dying.

He glanced at the puffy white clouds dotting the sky. *God, why do I feel as though You're up to something here?*

Lowering his gaze, he tightened his grip on the steering wheel and eased on the gas. That cow had to be around here somewhere.

He urged the UTV back to the pasture and had just rounded the edge of the woods when something caught his eye. Moving his foot to the brake, he narrowed his gaze as the black angus stood abruptly. There behind it lay a brand-spankin'-new black calf, its furry hide still moist.

Justin couldn't help smiling. He'd always been a sucker for babies. "Good job, mama."

With that, he turned the steering wheel and took off in the opposite direction. He hadn't gotten far when the Ky line vibrated in his pocket. Strange. She and Gloriana had only been gone an hour.

Bringing the UTV to a stop, he tapped the screen before pressing the phone to his ear. "Don't tell me y'all are giving up already."

"It's Ms. Gloriana!" His daughter's voice held a note of panic. "She was picking berries around a tree, and a copperhead bit her on the hand."

His body tensed. He ground his teeth, unwilling to think about the last phone call he'd received informing him someone he cared about was in danger.

Copperhead bites aren't deadly, he reminded himself. Though they were quite painful, tended to cause a fair amount of swelling and could cause tissue damage, particularly if they got infected.

"Where are you?" He stared across the pasture, trying to douse the helplessness sparking inside him.

"Grand pasture. Near Hickory Ridge."

That was the opposite side of the property. He couldn't get any farther away from them if he'd tried.

"If she's wearing any rings or a watch on that hand, tell her to take them off now before the swelling starts."

He listened as she repeated his instructions to Gloriana.

"Okay." Ky's breaths came in rapid succession. "Now what?"

"Y'all have Francie's UTV, right?"

"Uh, huh."

"Do you remember how to drive it?"

"Yeah."

"Good. Tell Gloriana to avoid any unnecessary or hurried movements, but get her into the passenger side." Despite the frenzy rising within, he managed to keep his voice calm. "Then I want you to drive her as quickly yet safely as you can back to Francie's. Can you do that for me?"

"I think so."

"I'll meet you there and take Gloriana to the hospital in Brenham."

Twenty-five minutes later, after stopping by the cabin to swap his UTV for his truck, he pulled up to Francie's house, where she hurried out to meet him, her steps determined, a leather bag dangling from one hand. He'd called her on his way back to let her know what had happened just in case the girls arrived before he did.

Her brow pinched as she peered up at him. "You're sure you don't mind taking her to the hospital?" While it was no secret he wasn't a fan of hospitals, he wasn't about to put any undue stress on Francie. A month after her surgery, she was finally acting more like her old self, and he didn't want any setbacks.

"As long as you don't mind Ky staying here."

The woman waved a hand. "Never."

The low groan of an engine captured their attention.

Justin turned to see Francie's UTV coming up the drive, a cloud of dust in its wake.

"Here's Glory's purse." She shoved it into Justin's hand. "She'll need her ID and such."

Looking down at Francie, he said, "I'll call you as soon as I know something."

Minutes later, he assisted a seemingly dazed Gloriana into the passenger side of his truck. She cradled her wrist in her good hand.

"How are you feeling?" He eyed her as they made their way onto the farm to market road.

Her gaze fixed on the pavement, she said, "It hurts." She didn't appear anxious, though she didn't act like she was all there, either.

A few minutes later, he slowed to maneuver a curve before cutting a glance her way. Her eyes were closed.

He could feel the unease building in his chest. "Gloriana?" He nudged her with his hand. "Hey."

Her head rolled toward his, and her eyes briefly opened. "Tired."

The horrific memories he'd been fending off since Ky's call blazed to the forefront of his mind. It had been five o'clock and he'd just gotten off work. He'd climbed into his truck and promptly plugged his dead phone into the charger, recalling Barbie's insistence that he upgrade to a newer model because his wouldn't hold a charge. A couple minutes later, the device binged and bonged as alerts of missed calls and texts appeared on the screen. Some from Barbie, others from Ky's school wanting to know if someone was coming to pick her up.

Now, his grip tightened on the steering wheel as his thoughts continued to drift. Barbie had gone on a field trip with Ky's class that day. Because of her type one diabetes, she always carried her insulin with her. That day, though, she'd somehow missed it when she changed purses. She was at the zoo when she discovered she didn't have it, and since she'd ridden the bus with the kids, she'd called him, asking if he could bring it to her.

Except he didn't get that message or the dozen that followed until he got off work. Along with one from the hospital. Apparently, after the kids returned to the school, Barbie drove herself to the hospital, hoping to get the insulin her body desperately needed. It was too late, though. She collapsed in the emergency room. By the time he got to the hospital, she was unconscious and never woke up.

Approaching the city of Brenham, he pushed the speed limit boundaries, determined to get Gloriana the help she needed. A short time later, he screeched to a halt outside the emergency room and threw the vehicle into Park before rushing around to her side and scooping her and her purse into his arms.

"I need help," he cried as he ran through the sliding doors.

The handful of people in the waiting room glanced his way while someone behind the desk called for a gurney. He rushed through an explanation of what happened before transferring her limp body onto the gurney. She was as pale as the white sheet beneath her.

"Sir, I'll need some information. Are you related to the patient?"

He stared at the woman with a clipboard. "No, just a friend." Though in that moment it became clear he wanted to be so much more. But he couldn't do it. He couldn't risk falling in love and losing someone ever again.

Chapter Ten

Two days later, Gloriana gripped the television remote in her left hand, grateful to finally be home. How did people ever get any rest in a hospital when there were nurses and technicians running in and out of one's room at all hours? Besides, the recliner in Mom's family room was far more comfortable than that hospital bed.

While her mother putzed in the kitchen, Gloriana flipped through the channels on the flat screen above the limestone fireplace. Uncomfortable, she adjusted her still-puffy right arm, casting an annoyed glance at the bevy of black lines and numbers that had served to monitor her swelling. Once upon a time, she'd been able to spot a snake from a mile away. Obviously being away from the ranch had dimmed her abilities.

She drew in an exasperated breath that carried the aroma of something sweet. Better that she'd gotten bit than Kyleigh, though. Not only would Gloriana hate for the girl to have to endure that kind of pain, she could just imagine how frantic poor Justin would've been.

A smile teased the corners of her mouth as she recalled the tender look on his face as he'd helped her into his truck. If only it had lasted. As her blood pressure dipped and she fought to stay awake on the way to the hospital, she'd glimpsed a deep ache in the hard lines etched on his face. The kind of pain that radiated from one's soul.

And then later, after they'd pumped her full of antivenin and antibiotics and transferred her to a regular room, she finally got to see him again. But he'd seemed so…distant, both physically and emotionally. He'd hovered near the doorway, awkwardly asking how she felt and insisting she needed to rest. Then he'd disappeared, and she hadn't seen him since.

Perhaps she was being overly sensitive. After all, he had Kyleigh to think about. And there were some people in this world who simply didn't do well in hospitals, no matter what the case. So she should just be grateful that he'd offered to take her instead of leaving that task to her mother. Mom certainly wasn't ready to be driving that far yet. So it had pleased Gloriana when Bill accompanied her mother to the hospital both yesterday and earlier today.

But try as she might, Gloriana couldn't ignore the ache in her heart.

Whether it was that night at Hideaway Cove when Justin had seemed to come to her defense as she told him about Cody leaving, or when he'd helped her clean the kitchen after Sunday dinner, making a chore feel like anything but. Or maybe it was the way he never hesitated to contact the board whenever she had some new idea. Whatever the case, somewhere in all that, she'd cracked open the door to her heart. Enough to allow a few what-ifs to sneak in and wreak havoc.

She should have known better. Now it was time to slam that door and lock it tight before she found herself brokenhearted once again.

The enticing aromas wafting from the kitchen made her stomach growl. "What are you making in there, Mom?"

"You'll find out soon enough." Moments later, her mother rounded the corner, holding a small plate topped with three ball-shaped objects coated in powdered sugar.

Gloriana's mouth dropped open. "Are those what I think they are?"

Mom settled the plate on the side table between the two recliners. "I assume Mexican wedding cookies are still your favorite."

"Yes, but you only make them at Christmas."

"Sweetheart, after all you've done for me these past few weeks, you deserve to be spoiled a little." Her mother's praise had Gloriana's heart swelling with joy. "It's been such a blessing to have you here. I can hardly bear the thought of you leaving." Mom sniffed.

Gloriana felt her own eyes welling. "Now you're going to make me cry." She swiped a wayward tear from her cheek. "And we've got work to do."

"Work?" Her mother scowled. "I think not. The rodeo will just have to wait."

"Your wedding won't, though. We've barely done anything. It's time to start making some lists."

"That can wait until you're feeling better."

"I am feeling better. And I've got my tablet and some cookies, though I might need more of those. So why don't you fix yourself a cuppa something and join me so we can start nailing down a few things."

"And here I thought *I* was bossy." Mom winked before disappearing into the kitchen again.

Gloriana turned off the television and grabbed her tablet, along with a cookie. Specks of powdered sugar peppered her black yoga pants as she took her first bite.

"Mmm..." She closed her eyes as the buttery treat melted on her tongue and the pecans awakened her taste buds.

"I'm surprised Justin hasn't been by yet." Holding her coffee mug in one hand, Mom placed a larger plate of cookies next to the first one before handing Gloriana a napkin. "We told him you were coming home today."

"What does that have to do with anything?"

"Don't think I haven't noticed how much time the two of you have been spending together lately." Easing into the opposite chair, Mom lifted a suspicious brow. "Surely it's not *always* about the rodeo."

Gloriana had to hide her smile as she thought about the fun times she'd had with Justin and Kyleigh. "You're forgetting that I'm also coaching his daughter." She grabbed another cookie. "But I will admit I enjoy Justin's company."

Her mother watched her curiously. "Oh, I have a feeling it's not just his company that puts that sparkle in your eye whenever he's around."

Gloriana set the cookie on her napkin without taking a bite. "Mom, when was the last time you heard me mention that I had a boyfriend or was dating someone?"

"Not since Cody, I suppose. But then, we didn't talk all that often. And when we did, you tended to be rather tight-lipped."

A fact that was sad but true. Sucking in a breath, Gloriana leaned her head back and stared at the ceiling fan. "There are only two men I have ever loved, and they both rejected me. I don't want to feel that kind of pain ever again."

Her mother's warm hand gently touched Gloriana's swollen arm. "Baby, your daddy loved you the best he could."

"By buying me things? Placating me?" She looked at her mother. "I never wanted all the stuff. I wanted him.

To feel like I was worthy of his time and attention. He and Hawkins were always laughing and having fun together. And I'm sorry if this sounds horrible, because you taught me a lot of good things over the years, but he was always pawning me off on you." Unexpected tears fell as she bared her soul to her mother for the first time. "I wasn't allowed to go hunting with him but, boy, I could cook up some fine chicken-fried venison." She couldn't help the sarcasm in her tone.

Wiping away the tears that now flowed freely down her cheeks, she continued, "Even Hawkins saw it. The poor guy was constantly trying to get Daddy to include me. Then Hawkins would apologize and offer to take me hunting or fishing."

Mom stood and came to kneel beside Gloriana's chair. "Except it wasn't the event you wanted. You wanted your daddy's attention. And you were determined to get it any way you could. Good or bad." Her mother's tone held an air of understanding tinged with regret.

Gloriana nodded as her mother stroked her hair.

"I don't know why I never saw it before. Or maybe I did and chose to ignore it." Mom touched Gloriana's chin, coaxing her to look at her. "You know you were our little miracle baby." Gloriana had been born three months premature. "Two-point-six pounds of sheer determination. Your daddy was afraid to hold you for fear he'd hurt you." Mom's smile was a sad one. "While I spent weeks at the hospital with you, he stayed home with Hawkins."

"Did he ever come and visit me?"

Her mother's countenance fell as she grabbed Gloriana's hand and slowly shook her head. "In his defense, he was afraid of growing attached and then losing you.

You had a couple of close calls. And he certainly had his hands full here at home.

"Your brother was only four, yet somehow your daddy managed to juggle both him and the ranch. Hawkins was always at his side, just as Boyd had done with his father."

"Is that supposed to make me feel better, Mom?"

Her mother cupped her face. "You may have been a girl, but you are more like your daddy than your brother will ever be. I believe you intimidated your father."

"Because I was so tiny?"

"At first. But you also weren't afraid." She cocked her head. "Did you know I had to talk him into letting you try barrel racing?"

Gloriana felt her eyes widen. "I thought it was his idea. I mean, I talked about it all the time, pestering y'all to no end. He always ignored me, though. Until that day he came to me and said, 'If you want to do barrel racing, we'd best get you a proper horse.'"

Mom chuckled. "I'd convinced him that once you saw how much dedication it took, you'd probably give up."

"You thought I'd give up?" Gloriana wasn't sure how she felt about that.

Mom contemplated her for a moment. "Honestly, I wasn't sure. But we never would've known if we hadn't let you try. I think that was when your daddy finally started looking at you as the strong young lady you'd become instead of the frail infant he'd placated all her life. And he wasn't quite sure what to do with that knowledge. Or with you."

Mom brushed Gloriana's hair away from her face the way she used to when Gloriana was a little girl. "Glory, your daddy might've had a hard time showing it, but he loved you every bit as much as he did your brother. I just wish he'd had more time to make it up to you."

"And I wish I'd had the opportunity to say goodbye."

"We all did, baby. Who would've guessed that when he went to bed that night, he'd never wake up?" Taking hold of Gloriana's hand again, Mom said, "We've all made mistakes. But I am so grateful for this time we have now. You gave up your job to take care of *me*. That's forced me to take a good look at myself. I know I've made my share of missteps along the way, but I really like where we are right now. And I hope my getting married doesn't change that."

Gloriana's phone interrupted them.

Mom hurried to retrieve it from the table, along with a couple of tissues, then handed them to Gloriana.

"It's my agent," said Gloriana. After blowing her nose, she answered. "Hi, Marlena."

"I know you said you're not interested in job hunting until closer to June, however, I've gotten an inside scoop on a potential newscaster position in Houston that would be perfect for you."

After the conversation she'd just had with her mother, Gloriana was having a hard time shifting gears. "Um, yeah. Houston would be great. However, I have some commitments here in Hope Crossing that I have yet to fulfill."

"That's all right. What I've shared is still hearsay at the moment, but I wanted to make you aware so you could be thinking about it. Opportunities like this don't come along every day. And this one has your name written all over it. A top ten market and close to home, which is what you said you wanted." Actually, it was Marlena who'd been hoping for the larger market.

But Gloriana let it go. "Yes, it certainly fits my parameters." Too bad she wasn't more excited about it. A few months ago she would have jumped at this kind of opportunity. And it met the criteria she'd given Marlena less than two weeks ago. So what was the problem?

As everything that had transpired since that call played through her mind, Gloriana found herself wondering if living close enough to come home would be enough. Or was it, perhaps, that she actually wanted to *be* home? And did a certain ranch manager who seemed to be avoiding her play a role in her indecision?

Justin trudged into Plowman's Thursday afternoon, feeling rougher than he had in a long time. After what he'd experienced Tuesday, he knew he had no choice but to keep his distance from Gloriana. It was the only way to guard his heart. And while he also knew it was for the best, he'd been miserable ever since.

He grabbed a loaf of bread, realizing that somewhere along the way, he'd started thinking of Gloriana as more than just a friend, entertaining notions he had no business inviting to the party in the first place. A fact that became crystal clear as he'd carried her seemingly lifeless body into the hospital and gave him the wake-up call he'd needed. A stern reminder that he was better off keeping his heart in check so he'd never have to experience the pain of loss ever again.

And how's that working out for you?

Groaning, he snagged a couple of Dr Peppers from the cooler. Better to nip things in the bud now. Gloriana wasn't going to stay in Hope Crossing forever. Once Francie married and the rodeo was over, she'd be gone, back to some big city and a career that didn't even exist in Hope Crossing. So he'd do well to keep things between them strictly business.

After grabbing a package of Ky's favorite chips and some peanut butter cups, he paid the cashier and headed for the high school. As usual, his daughter was talking with a group of friends when he drove up. She smiled when she spotted him. Most days, she lingered a minute or two, finishing whatever conversation they were having, but that wasn't the case today. She practically rushed the truck before he even brought it to a stop.

"Is Ms. Gloriana home?" Her grin stretched from ear to ear as she pulled the passenger door closed and buckled her seat belt. "How is she?"

"According to Bill, she came home late this morning." He slowly followed the throng of vehicles out of the parking lot. "And she's happy to be out of the hospital."

"Wait." Ky twisted to face him. "So you haven't gone to check on her?"

Turning onto the main road, he said, "She's still recovering. She doesn't need a bunch of visitors."

"How can you say that? I was with her when she got bit. You saved her life, driving her to the hospital."

He cut a glance toward the passenger seat. "I did not save her life."

"You don't know that." She crossed her arms and flopped back against the seat in a huff. "She's going to think we don't care."

Justin groaned. There was the crux of the problem. He did care. Too much. If he didn't, he wouldn't have had such a hard time staying away from Francie's house today.

Country music filled the cab of the truck as Ky remained silent, barely touching her soda and completely ignoring the snacks he'd bought. At least until they pulled into the drive of Prescott Farms.

"I *want* to see Ms. Gloriana."

He looked in her direction to see her bottom lip pooched out and unshed tears threatening to spill onto her rosy cheeks at any moment.

"Ky." He reached for her, but she jerked away.

"Ms. Gloriana is my friend, and I care about her."

"I know you do." And that terrified him. She'd grown attached to Gloriana, too. Sure, he'd find some way to muddle through when Gloriana left, but what about Ky? How would losing another person she cared about impact her?

"If I was the one who'd gotten bit, she'd come to see me. Probably even bring me cookies or something."

He couldn't argue with her there. "Okay, I'll drop you off." He veered to the right, following the gravel road toward Francie's instead of the cabin.

Stopping in the circular drive, he said, "You can text when you're ready for me to pick you up."

"No, Daddy. You have to come, too."

Tilting his hat back, he scrubbed a hand over his face. Ky rarely called him *Daddy* anymore. So when she did, he found himself almost helpless to say no.

"All right, fine." He killed the engine and opened the door. Rounding the truck, he added, "No more than ten minutes."

She clapped her hands, hurried onto the porch and knocked enthusiastically.

Moments later, a smiling Francie opened the door. "I've been wondering if we'd see you today." She stepped back, allowing them to enter.

"Is Ms. Gloriana here?" His daughter bounced on the balls of her sneaker-clad feet.

Justin set a hand on her shoulder. "The better question would be, is she up to having visitors?"

"Yes, I am," came a voice from the other room.

Wearing her biggest smile yet, Ky bolted in that direction, leaving him to shake his head while Francie eased the door closed.

"Oh, to have that much energy," the older woman said. "She reminds me of Gloriana when she was that age."

Hoping she wouldn't catch on to the fact that he was trying to buy some time, he met her dark gaze. "And how are you doing?"

"You know what?" She smiled. "After being the needy one for these past weeks, it's good to feel needed again."

That was Francie, all right. Always taking care of others.

"In that case, how is Gloriana doing?"

She gestured toward the family room. "Why don't you see for yourself?"

He could hear Ky jabbering up a storm as he made his way across the tile floor. As he stepped into the family room, Gloriana lifted her gaze, her hazel eyes sparkling when they connected with his. Her long tresses were piled on top of her head in a messy-yet-oh-so-appealing way, and her smile reached past each and every one of his defenses.

Suddenly, the distance he'd hoped to maintain seemed impossible. In the battle between his head and his heart, his heart had taken the lead. And by the time they all finished dinner a couple hours later, he no longer cared.

Gloriana smiled, watching Ky gather the empty plates after they'd devoured Francie's fabulous chicken spa-

ghetti. "First Mom makes my favorite cookies, then
my favorite dinner." She set her napkin aside, glancing
around the table. "I need to hurry up and move past this
snakebite, otherwise I'll never fit into my clothes."

"Nonsense." Francie waved a hand. "If I know you,
you barely touched that hospital food, so you were simply catching up."

"Whatever you say, Mom." Gloriana scooted her chair
back. "I think I'd like to step outside for a bit and get
some fresh air. I've been cooped up all day."

Justin hurried out of his own chair to help her.

Peering up at him, she smiled and placed her good
hand in his. "Thank you."

He couldn't ignore the heat rushing up his arm.

"Justin, why don't you accompany Gloriana while
Kyleigh and I clean up the kitchen? I'd hate for her to be
out there alone."

Eyeing the woman whose slender fingers still rested
in his palm, he smiled. "Not a problem."

After confirming the chickens were in their pen, he
led Gloriana out onto the patio.

The sun was still above the horizon, and a gentle
breeze rustled the leaves on the large oak tree in the
corner of the yard.

Gloriana took a deep breath. "It's so nice to breathe
antiseptic-free air."

He couldn't help but chuckle. "You'll get no argument
here." Still holding her hand, he moved in front of her.
"Look, I'm, uh, sorry for the way I bolted on you Tuesday."

"It was getting late. You needed to get home to
Kyleigh."

"That's not why I left." He cleared his throat. "I left
because I was scared. When you lost consciousness on

the way to the hospital, it brought back a lot of memories. Memories I'd rather forget."

Her eyes searched his as she squeezed his hand. "When your wife died?"

Looking away, he nodded.

"Do you mind if I ask what happened?" Her voice was soft. Tentative. "How did she die?"

Turning, he stared out over the horizon. "Ketoacidosis. I mentioned before that she was diabetic." Forcing himself to meet Gloriana's gaze again, he quietly told her about the day his whole world fell apart. He found it strange, though, that it didn't feel quite as painful as it had the other night.

"If my phone hadn't died, if I'd just gotten her message, maybe my daughter wouldn't have lost her mother."

"You're being awful hard on yourself." She lifted her hand to cup his cheek. "Bad things happen. Things we may never understand. But you shouldn't blame yourself."

"But don't you see? The phone was old. It wasn't holding a charge. If I'd replaced it like she kept telling me—" He shook his head, causing her hand to fall away, and he instantly missed her touch.

"That's why you carry two phones, isn't it?" Her expression was filled with tenderness as she again reached for his hand.

Afraid to speak, he simply nodded. Looking into her eyes, he glimpsed something he'd all but given up on. Hope. Hope that, perhaps, he wasn't destined to walk through life alone. That maybe he could care for someone else. That, by the grace of God, he might be able to love again.

Chapter Eleven

Perhaps that snakebite hadn't been such a bad thing, after all.

Gloriana sat at the dining room table–turned–desk, amazed at all the things she'd managed to cross off her ever-growing to-do list this past week. Now that her mother was pretty much back to normal and self-sufficient, Gloriana had utilized her downtime to make sure every *i* was dotted and every *t* crossed regarding Mom's wedding and the rodeo. Gloriana wanted both to be a success, which meant she couldn't afford to let anything slip through the cracks.

Since this would be a second marriage for both her mother and Bill, they'd decided to have the wedding and reception in the backyard with a good ol' Texas barbecue theme. Not a bad idea, since they'd chosen to exchange their vows the Saturday before Memorial Day. That alone had Gloriana a little worried about locking in party rentals and catering, but God had orchestrated everything perfectly, so her worry had been for naught. Even the flowers and cake had been selected and ordered. The only major thing still on the list was to find dresses for the bride and her daughter, aka the maid of honor. That could be their greatest challenge of all, though.

She checked her watch. Justin would be picking her up for supper in an hour. They'd spent an incredible amount of time together this past week, and she found herself looking forward to seeing him. Something had changed since he'd shared the details of his wife's death. Not only did he smile more, but morning coffee together had become a daily ritual. Lunch, too. And tonight wouldn't be the first time she'd had dinner at the cabin with him and Kyleigh. Though Justin always insisted on being her escort, refusing to let her drive yet, despite the fact that she was perfectly capable. And while she was still waiting for him to kiss her, the looks he gave her sometimes were every bit as exciting.

Mom said it sounded like good, old-fashioned courting. All Gloriana knew was that she'd never had a man pursue her like this. And while there was no doubt she was enjoying it, she was also terrified. What if Justin changed his mind about her the way Cody had? And what about her career? One that had seemed to be gaining momentum. One she'd worked hard to achieve. One that no longer held the allure it once had.

She let out a sigh. While she once thrived on the competition, now she was more interested in building relationships. Promoting the rodeo, knowing she was helping kids live out their dreams—not to mention drawing attention to the community, which, she hoped, would translate to more revenue—gave her a sense of satisfaction that had been missing from her life. Even something as simple as working with Kyleigh brought her more joy than she'd felt in years.

The doorbell rang, interrupting her musing. The way

Justin had been behaving lately, she wouldn't be surprised if he'd decided to show up early. Though she was nowhere near ready.

Since her mother had already gone to Bill's for the evening, Gloriana stood and padded to the door in her bare feet. But it wasn't Justin who stood on the other side. It was Brady. Wearing his deputy's uniform, no less.

A sense of dread skittered up her spine. Not that she'd done anything wrong, she just couldn't imagine why he'd come here.

With a quick prayer, she swung open the door, trying not to let her nerves get the best of her. "Brady?" Still clinging to the door, she allowed her gaze to roam from his thick hair to his booted feet and back. "What can I do for you?"

"Ignore the uniform. I'm here on official rodeo board business."

What, were they going to fire her?

Taking a step back, she said, "Would you care to come in?"

He moved inside. "Charlene received a phone call from the Texas Pit Masters group."

Closing the door, Gloriana faced him again. "That's the barbecue association that pulled out of the fair and rodeo, right? What did they want?"

"Seems a twister in east Texas last week wiped out part of the fairgrounds where they were supposed to hold one of their competitions. It's been canceled, so they're looking for an alternative and heard we've got all sorts of good things going on at this year's Hope Crossing Fair and Rodeo."

She crossed her arms, feeling more than a little satisfied that they'd come crawling back. "With all the promotion we've done, I'm sure they have. So what did Charlene tell them?"

"That we'd require a three-year commitment."

Gloriana couldn't help smiling. "Nicely done, Charlene." She peered up at her old friend. "So how come you're here telling me and not her?" Then again, Charlene pretty much hated her.

"Because I wanted to say thank you for all you've done. You've likely saved our fair and rodeo. And you've reminded the board, if not the whole town, what we once had and why it was so special."

She swallowed around the sudden lump in her throat. "I still believe in Clay's dream. And I want other kids to have those same opportunities that you and I did."

His piercing blue eyes seemed to bore into her for the longest time. "You really have changed."

She allowed her arms to fall to her sides. "Thanks for noticing."

Dropping his gaze, he said, "I need to run." He reached for the door. Pulled it open. "I just wanted to make you aware of the change. Hope it doesn't mess up anything."

"Nah. It's just one more thing folks will have to look forward to."

A sense of relief washed over her as she closed the door and slumped against it. She'd just received the closest thing to forgiveness she'd probably ever hear from Brady.

Her phone buzzed on the table. Hurrying to grab it, she saw Justin's name on the screen. Her heart skipped a beat as she opened his text. So not like her.

Are you ready for me to pick you up?

She checked her watch. "Yikes." She still needed to change.

I'll be ready in fifteen. She hit Send.

The appreciative look he gave her when she opened the door *fourteen* minutes later had her insides doing all sorts of weird gyrations. Since when had she responded like that to any man? In recent history, anyway.

As soon as she'd pulled the door closed, Justin reached for her hand, sending a thrill all the way to her toes. They moved from the porch onto the sidewalk.

"So what are Francie and Bill up to tonight?"

"They're at his place, discussing redecorating."

Justin chuckled. "Poor fella."

"I think it's sweet that he's allowing her to make the place her own." Since Bill had his own ranch to look after while Mom had Justin to oversee Prescott Farms, it made sense for her mother to move to Bill's. And the fact that he was open to change revealed just how much he loved her.

"You're right." Reaching the circular drive, he paused near the passenger side of his truck while a couple of wrens chirped in the tree overhead. "Love can make a guy do all sorts of crazy things."

"Oh, really." Tilting her head to peer up at him, she said, "Such as?"

The intensity of his gaze surprised her. And she couldn't help her sharp intake of breath when he cupped her cheek and threaded his fingers into her hair.

Goose flesh peppered her arms. Her heart raced as he leaned closer.

Finally, his lips brushed over hers. So soft and warm, making her feel more than just wanted, but cherished.

All too soon, he pulled away, though his gorgeous eyes remained fixed on hers.

Her lips still tingling, she said, "I'm good with crazy."

Smiling, he slid his other arm around her waist and pulled her closer before kissing her again.

She wound her arms around his neck, wanting to stay in this moment forever. But Kyleigh was waiting.

When they finally parted, he grinned, reaching for the door. "Hungry?"

As if she could think about food after a kiss like that. "Starving."

Neither said a word as they pulled away from the house. Was Justin as stunned by this latest turn of events as she was? Her mind was reeling. Thoughts of being held in his arms were definitely going to keep her awake tonight.

Then her brain kicked in. "Oh, I forgot to tell you." She eyed him across the cab as they rolled down the drive a few minutes later. "Remember me mentioning the barbecue cook-off that had always been a part of the fair and rodeo?"

"I do." He eyed the horses in the pasture adjacent the barn.

"They want to come back." She went on to explain the details.

"With the event you've created, I wouldn't be surprised if folks started crawling out of the woodwork, wanting to come and join us."

"You're sweet to say that."

He wound onto the narrow drive that led to the cabin. "Gloriana, I wasn't trying to be sweet or to flatter you. At least not this time." He winked, making her feel all warm and fuzzy inside. "You've put together something none of us ever even thought possible. I mean, you've got

Luke Phillips coming to Hope Crossing. Do you think anyone else on the board could've pulled that off?"

As they came to a stop in front of the cabin, she said, "Point taken. I just don't want people thinking anything I did was to bring attention to myself. At one time, perhaps, but not now. My only desire is for the rodeo to be a success."

He reached for her hand and gave it a squeeze. "I know. And I have every confidence that it will be."

The aroma of garlic greeted them when Justin opened the door to the cabin minutes later.

"Y'all are just in time." Behind the counter, Kyleigh smiled and continued slicing a narrow loaf of buttery garlic bread. "You can go ahead and sit down."

Justin pulled out one of four spindled barrel chairs for Gloriana. "She insisted on preparing the entire meal herself," he whispered.

"She's had plenty of practice."

After Justin said grace, they eagerly dug into their meal.

"I still can't believe the rodeo is only five weeks away." Kyleigh twirled her fork in the spaghetti.

"This is a first." Justin grabbed another slice of garlic bread. "You're counting down to the rodeo instead of your birthday."

She sent her father a look. "It's not like fifteen is a big deal. At least, not when my first rodeo is coming up."

"According to my mother—" Gloriana stabbed at her salad "—every birthday is a big deal." Her fork hovered over her bowl, ranch dressing dripping from her lettuce. "When is it?"

"June third." While Kyleigh behaved as if the day had

no special significance, Gloriana nearly choked on her romaine.

Coughing, she reached for her water.

"Are you okay?" Justin moved beside her, no doubt ready to perform the Heimlich maneuver.

Gloriana held up a hand. "I'm—" she covered another cough with her napkin "—fine." She took a drink, her heart pounding like a horse's hooves in a full gallop. June third was the day she'd given birth to a beautiful dark-haired baby girl. A child that would turn fifteen this year.

She drew a shuddering breath. "Sorry about that."

"You're sure you're okay?" Justin's concerned gaze remained on her.

"Yes."

Embarrassment washed over her as he returned to his seat. Talk about overreacting. So Kyleigh shared a birthday with her baby. The notion of Kyleigh being that child was ridiculous. After all, Justin had said he and Barbie had lived in the DFW area. Gloriana had given birth in Lubbock. There must have been countless children born in Texas on that date.

But how many were given up for adoption?

Justin wound his truck into Francie's drive a little before nine.

"Hmm." Gloriana eyed the darkened house. "It doesn't look like Mom's made it home yet."

"Are you worried?" He eased the vehicle to a stop and put it in Park.

"No, just a little surprised." She faced him now, the full moon shining through the windshield, illuminating her beautiful face. "Come to think of it, though, this is the first time she's gone to Bill's since I've been home. With Mom's recovery, he's always come over here."

"Speaking of recoveries, tonight wasn't too much for you, was it? I wasn't anticipating Ky would ask you to help with her homework."

"I'm fine." She waved a hand. "Besides, I don't think I helped her all that much. She's a smart kid. A little moral support was all she needed."

"I think she enjoys your attention." Not that he could blame his daughter. He'd found himself wanting more of Gloriana's attention, too.

His mind wandered back to the kiss they'd shared. He was pretty sure it had taken them both by surprise. Yet it felt so right. And the way she'd responded had him walking on air ever since. Even now, he couldn't stop thinking about the sweet smell of her hair and how perfectly she fit in his arms.

He never thought he'd have feelings for anyone other than Barbie. Now he was falling for Gloriana. And it seemed like the most natural thing in the world.

"Are you planning anything special for her birthday?" Her voice drew him out of his thoughts.

"Ky's?" He shrugged. "It's usually just the two of us. Sometimes your mom. She always makes Ky a cake."

Gloriana smiled. "Of course. That's what Francie does."

"Maybe I should consider doing something different this year." He shook his head. "She's growing up so fast. I feel like my time with her is running out."

Reaching across the center console, Gloriana rested her hand on his arm. "From what I've seen, you and Kyleigh have a very special relationship. Just because she's growing up doesn't mean that's going to go away.

It'll simply grow, too." Her words warmed his heart and chased his fears away.

He twisted to face her, setting his hand atop hers in hopes she wouldn't pull away. "Maybe you could help me plan her birthday."

"Oh…" Her gaze shifted to something outside the windshield. "I don't know about that." She tried to pull away, but he held tight.

"I'm sorry. I wasn't thinking. With your mom's wedding the weekend prior and the fair and rodeo the following weekend, you're not going to have time for anything else that week."

She looked at him. "I'll always have time for Kyleigh."

"I know. But I worry about you. You've been crazy busy, even after the snakebite. You need to take care of yourself." He squeezed her hand. "If there's anything I can do to alleviate some of your burden or make you smile—"

She did just that. "How about walking me to the door?"

And just when things were getting cozy. "Your wish is my command." He turned off the engine, exited and met her on the other side of the truck.

The sounds of crickets and katydids echoed through the night air as they strolled up the walk.

"So what is Francie going to do with this house when she moves in with Bill?"

"Let's see," said Gloriana, "she's talked about renting, both long term and as a vacation-type rental. City people love the idea of escaping to the country for a weekend or more."

They might, but he certainly wasn't fond of the idea.

"She's mentioned offering it to you and Kyleigh."

He shook his head as they stepped onto the porch. "This is way too big for just the two of us."

"Of course, I'll stay here for a while. Until I learn where my next job will land me."

It wasn't that long ago he couldn't wait for Gloriana to leave. Now the thought of not seeing her everyday twisted his insides.

"I told my agent I'll only look at prospects within driving distance of Prescott Farms, so I can come home more often." Her half-hearted shrug encouraged him. "Rumor has it there might be an opening soon at one of the Houston stations, which is about the best I could hope for in terms of proximity. That is, assuming it's something I'm interested in and can land."

"Why do I get the impression this is something you feel like you have to do but don't necessarily *want* to do?"

Under the porch light, she stared up at him. "It's what I always wanted to do. What I've done most of my adult life."

"Does it make you happy?"

She looked away. "It used to."

"What about now?"

She continued to stare at something in the night. "It's a demanding job. And I've thrived in that environment for more than a decade. But since coming back here…" Finally, she faced him again. "I've seen a whole lot of things I've been missing out on."

He saw the confusion in her eyes. "You could stay here." Nodding toward the house, he added, "You've already got a place to live."

"But what would I do out here? How would I make a living? Broadcasting is all I know. It's the only thing I've ever done."

"Are you kidding me? Look at all the stuff you've done for the rodeo. You tapped into your skills to promote it all across the state. You've used your connections to bring in rodeo and country music stars. And you did it all without ever setting foot out of Hope Crossing."

"My efforts for the rodeo have been gratis. That won't pay the bills."

"But you're full of ideas that can help others. Remember what you said about the dance hall and renting it for another source of income? You're the perfect person to make that happen. And with your marketing ideas, I wouldn't be surprised to see it booked up in no time."

"Justin—"

He held up a hand. "Let me finish." He had no idea where his thoughts were coming from, but he was desperate enough to keep going. "There are small towns all across this region and they all have something to offer, but people who don't live there know nothing about them. What if you were to start your own advertising, marketing, promotion, whatever you call that kind of business and target small towns, helping them get the word out?"

She stared at him for the longest time, finally smiling. "You've certainly given me something to think about."

"Good." Because while he didn't know where his relationship with Gloriana was headed, he was willing to fight for it. Something he'd never had the opportunity to do with Barbie.

Lord, please don't let me mess this up. Please, let Gloriana stay.

Chapter Twelve

Gloriana stared at the ceiling in her bedroom the next morning. She'd barely slept last night, unable to stop thinking about Justin and that kiss. Not to mention all the ideas he'd thrown out, as though he wanted her to stay in Hope Crossing. Even now, his actions had her almost giddy.

Of course, those weren't the only things keeping her awake. Kyleigh's birth date was like a billboard flashing in her mind's eye. Now, the part of her that said "no way" was being drowned out by the what-ifs. Not to mention the offhanded remarks that had somehow surfaced in her memory. Patty pointing out the problem Kyleigh had with one of her turns, the same problem Gloriana always battled. Mom's comments of how Kyleigh reminded her of Gloriana. The fact that they were both left-handed.

But the thing that refused to let her go was Kyleigh's dark eyes. Gloriana had always thought there was something familiar about them, though she couldn't figure out what. But as she sat with her mother last night, listening to all the plans she and Bill had made for their future home, Gloriana realized she'd been staring into those same dark eyes since the day she was born.

Shaking her head, she wondered if she was simply imagining things. She needed to talk to someone before she drove herself crazy. And there was only one person who knew her secret. But with Tori being a teacher, she wouldn't be available until late this afternoon. Even then, she might be busy. As a working single mother, Tori's time was always in high demand.

Gloriana retrieved her phone from the nightstand and opened her messaging app.

I need to talk. Are you available later?

Her friend responded right away.

I'm available now. Aiden had a fever last night. Fever-free now but playing it safe.

Thankful she wouldn't have to wait, Gloriana typed again. Poor Aiden. See you soon. I'll bring kolaches.

Yum! Coffee will be waiting.

After texting Justin to let him know she'd have to pass on their usual morning coffee but would still meet him for lunch, Gloriana grabbed a quick shower, let her mother know her plans and then headed to Plowman's for some fresh-baked goodness before continuing on to Tori's.

Her friend still lived in the same house she'd grown up in, a charming sage-green folk Victorian with white trim and a picket fence, nestled in the piney woods west of town.

Gloriana was still wavering when she pulled into Tori's driveway. Maybe she was overthinking this whole birth-date thing. Trying to make a mountain out of a molehill, as her grandmother used to say.

She took a deep breath. *Lord, I need Your wisdom.*

Armed with the box of kolaches, she climbed the porch steps a few moments later, only to discover her friend waiting at the door. "Okay, what are you looking forward to the most? The kolaches or listening to me ramble?"

Tori smiled. "You, of course. When was the last time we were able to sit down for coffee on the spur of the moment?"

"Good point."

"Though the kolaches are a close second." Laughing at her own joke, Tori held the door wide, allowing Gloriana to pass. Dressed in cutoffs and a T-shirt with her blond hair twisted into a messy updo, her friend looked more like a teenager than a woman nearing her midthirties.

"How's Aiden?"

No sooner had the words left her mouth than the dark-haired toddler came racing into the living room wearing Spider-Man pajamas, his sock feet sliding across the longleaf-pine floor.

"Sweetie—" his frowning mother knelt to his level, "—you're supposed to be resting."

"I'm all done." His brown eyes peered at her so earnestly that Gloriana wondered how her friend ever managed to discipline the sweet child.

Tori released an exasperated sigh. "Tell you what, if you'll stay on the couch, I'll let you watch a movie." She glanced up at Gloriana. "Ms. Gloriana brought us some kolaches. Would you like me to cut one up for you?"

"Yes!" He threw his arms around his mother's neck, nearly knocking her over.

"He's so cute," Gloriana said as the two women took their seats at the kitchen table a short time later. "How can you ever bring yourself to punish him?"

Tori set her #1 Teacher mug on the whitewashed wood table. "Experience has helped me develop an immunity to cuteness. Most days, anyway." She grabbed a cream cheese–cherry kolache. "Thanks for remembering my favorite."

Gloriana took a peach one. "You're welcome."

"So what do we need to talk about?"

Setting her breakfast aside, she wrapped both hands around her coffee mug in an effort to warm her fingers while she debated where to start. Then decided to simply cut to the chase. "Justin's daughter, Kyleigh?"

"Sweet girl," Tori said as she chewed.

"Yes, she is. She's also adopted, and I found out last night that her birthday is June third. And she turns fifteen this year."

Her friend's blue eyes went wide. "Are you saying—"

"Frankly, I don't know what I'm saying. But ever since learning her birth date, I've had all these random tidbits of conversations and innocent remarks replaying in my mind."

"Such as?"

Gloriana listed them off.

"Wow. I never noticed it before, but now that you mention it, Kyleigh's eyes are very similar to your mother's."

"See, that's just it. We didn't see those things until after learning her birth date. So are we imagining it?"

"Yeah, I can see where it could go either way. Happenstance or reality." Tori picked up her mug. "So what are you going to do?"

"That's why I'm here. I was hoping you'd know."

"Oh, like I have all the answers." She sipped her coffee. "I haven't even dealt with my own reality."

Gloriana picked at her kolache. "I heard Micah is back in town." He and Tori had been close friends all through high school, until his older brother, Joel, came home on leave from the marines, swept Tori off her feet and married her a few months after she graduated.

"Yes. He separated from the marines and came home to help his mother." Tori took a deep breath. "It's awkward, though. We used to be so close." She looked at Gloriana. "Enough about that. We're here to talk about you."

"Me and my crazy, mixed-up life."

Tori rested her elbows on the table. "Let me ask you this. What if it turned out Kyleigh was your daughter? What would you do?"

"I don't know. I haven't thought that far ahead. I guess it wouldn't change much of anything. Justin is her father. I can't undo that, nor would I want to. I couldn't have handpicked a better father for her. And she and I would still be friends. Though I'd hope to grow our relationship. That is…" A wave of panic squeezed her chest. "What if she doesn't want anything to do with me? What if she's mad at me for giving her up? What if—"

"Don't go there." Tori held up a hand. "You're only going to make yourself crazy. Kyleigh is a levelheaded young lady. Actually, with her mother gone, I could see her being more open to building your relationship."

"Good point."

"By the way, how are things going between you and Justin?"

Gloriana couldn't help smiling as she again thought about that kiss.

"I know that look." Her friend leaned closer. "All right, Glory. Spill."

"What?"

"Oh, don't even. Your cheeks are as pink as can be."

Gloriana promptly covered them with her hands.

Tori's gaze narrowed. "You kissed him."

"I did not."

"You lie!"

"No, I'm not." She couldn't seem to stop grinning. "He kissed me."

"I knew it!" Her friend smacked the table with the palm of her hand.

"Mommy?"

Gloriana eyed the little boy over his mother's shoulder. "Busted."

Tori waved her son to her. "What is it, sweetie?"

He glanced at Gloriana.

She waved.

"You too wowd." His brown eyes moved from his mother to Gloriana and back again.

"Now you know how I feel when you and your friends are all shrieking in the nursery at church." Standing, she picked up the boy. "But Ms. Glory and I will try to do better, okay?" She carried him into the front room.

A few seconds later, she returned to her seat. "I think you need to tell Justin your suspicions. I mean, if you're going to have any kind of meaningful relationship, he needs to know about your past."

"That I had a baby."

"Yes."

"My own mother doesn't even know." Hawkins, either.

Tori reached for her hand. "You didn't do anything wrong, Gloriana. Cody was the one who turned his back on you and your baby. Meanwhile, you giving your child to a loving couple who couldn't have a baby of their own was probably the most selfless thing any woman could do."

"You don't know how many times I've told myself that very thing. But I've kept it a secret all these years. I know Mom is going to be hurt."

"She'll get over it. Besides, if it turns out you are Kyleigh's birth mother, just think of all Kyleigh would gain. A very special relationship with the woman who gave her life, and another grandmother. One can never have too many grandmas. And it's a role Francie would readily embrace."

"She sure would." Gloriana looked out the window to the massive pines standing sentry over the backyard. "But what if things don't work out with Justin?" She faced her friend again. "I will be going back to work at some point."

"Where?" Tori's brow pinched.

"I don't know yet. Houston is a possibility."

"That's almost an hour and a half away. More with traffic."

"It's not like I'm planning to commute."

"That's my point." Tori ripped off a piece of kolache and popped it in her mouth. "I wish you could stay in Hope Crossing."

Gloriana puffed a laugh. "Justin said the same thing."

As if on cue, her phone rang, and her agent's name appeared on the screen. "I need to take this." She tapped the screen. "Hello?"

"I have some wonderful news." Marlena's singsong voice only made Gloriana more nervous.

"Oh?" She eyed her friend.

"That position I told you about in Houston is now open, and they can't wait to interview you."

Gloriana couldn't seem to muster much enthusiasm. "When?"

"They have openings Monday, Tuesday and Wednesday next week. Just let me know which day and I'll take it from there."

She rested her forehead on her hand. This was too soon. She wasn't ready.

She wasn't sure if she'd ever be ready.

Justin pulled leftovers from the refrigerator while he waited for Gloriana to arrive, surprised at how quickly he'd grown accustomed to sharing lunch with her each day. His morning hadn't felt quite the same, either, not talking with her over coffee. Yeah, he enjoyed spending time with her, all right. Perhaps too much.

Ever since she'd brought up the notion of leaving last night, and then he'd frantically tried to convince her to stay, he'd been wondering if, maybe, things were moving too fast. If *he* was moving too fast. When she'd talked about finding another job, though, he'd suddenly felt as if his time with her was running out, and he was desperate to stop it. But how? He was just a simple guy. And while Gloriana might fit into his world, he'd never fit into hers.

He spooned some spaghetti onto a paper plate and had covered it with wax paper when he heard a vehicle coming up the drive. His traitorous heart raced with anticipation. *Gloriana.*

Smiling, he crossed into the living room and opened the front door as she brought her SUV to a stop. He continued off the porch as she got out and cast a wary glance in his direction. What was that about?

Meeting her midway between the porch and her vehicle, he dropped a brief kiss on her temple as though it was the most natural thing in the world. "You're driving again. Are you sure you're up to that?"

"I'm fine." Her smile was tremulous, like she was nervous about something. "Tori was home with Aiden today, and I wasn't about to miss out on an opportunity to visit with her."

"That's good that y'all were finally able to get together." They continued onto the porch, and he pushed the door open. "What would you prefer? Leftovers or a sandwich?"

She followed him inside, watching as he closed the door. "I'm not very hungry. I picked up some kolaches for me and Tori, so I'm kind of full."

Yet she still came to spend time with you! His heart smiled.

"You don't mind if I eat, do you?" He continued into the kitchen, where he moved his plate into the microwave.

"No, of course not." Her voice seemed different. Strained. "There's, um, something I need to talk to you about, though."

His gut tightened at the seemingly ominous words.

He punched the buttons on the microwave before turning to face her. "Is everything okay?"

"I think so." Again with the wobbly smile. "But there's something I need to tell you."

He shouldn't be nervous, but he was. Had she taken the job in Houston? Was she leaving even before the rodeo? Or maybe it was about him. In his panic last night, had he scared her away? Come across as too eager or over-bearing?

"Okay." He noticed the way she kept wringing her hands. This wasn't looking good. "Have a seat and I'll join you in a sec. Can I get you some water?" Yeah, he was trying to buy time.

Moving to the table, she said, "I'm good, thanks." She pulled out a chair and sat as he retrieved his meal from the microwave.

After setting it on the table in the spot beside her, he sat down, his body tense as he tried to pretend as though everything was normal. He said grace and grabbed his fork.

"So what's up?"

She drew in a long breath. "That night at Hideaway Cove."

He watched her, unable to touch his food, and not only because of the steam billowing off it.

"I told you about my husband walking out on me. That he said marrying me had been a mistake."

Why was she bringing that up again when it was obviously painful for her? "Gloriana, you don't have to rehash that. I know it wasn't easy for you the first time you spoke about it."

"No, it wasn't. Except I didn't tell you everything. I left off one—*the*—main reason he left me."

Seeing her struggle, Justin wanted to take her into his arms and tell her everything would be okay. Instead, he settled for saying, "I doubt I could think any less of him than I already do."

She nodded, worrying her bottom lip. Finally, "He left because I was pregnant, and he didn't want children."

Justin's blood began to boil. For a man to walk out on

his wife was bad enough, but to turn his back on her when she's pregnant? The sickened feeling in his gut was surpassed only by a strong urge to protect the woman beside him. He covered her hand with his, willing his feelings for her to wipe away all the pain and disappointment her husband had left behind.

"I never told anybody I was pregnant, except for Tori. Not even my family."

Pregnancy usually equated to a baby. But Gloriana didn't have a child. At least, not that he was aware of. Was that what she was trying to tell him? That she had a child hidden away somewhere?

He squeezed her hand. "What happened to your baby?"

For the moment, her anxiety seemed to wane. "I carried her to term. She was born right after I finished my sophomore year at Texas Tech. And then she was adopted by a wonderful couple who weren't able to have their own children."

"That couldn't have been easy. But you did the right thing."

She nodded, though her nervous twitching resumed when her eyes met his. "Justin, my baby girl was born the same day as Kyleigh."

He stared at her for the longest time as his mind raced back to that day he and Barbie received the call that the woman who had pledged her baby to them was in labor. They'd been beyond excited as they loaded Barbie's car with at least half of the baby paraphernalia they'd bought in anticipation of the arrival, then driven through the night so they could be at the hospital in Lubbock—the same town as Texas Tech—the moment their baby arrived.

He tried to swallow around the boulder that'd lodged in his throat. Was it possible the woman he was falling in love with was Ky's mother? Ky would be ecstatic. The two of them were already growing close. Unless…

His stomach churned. What if that had been Gloriana's plan all along? What if Ky was the real reason she came back home?

He extracted his hand from hers. This couldn't be happening. "What is it you're trying to tell me, Gloriana?"

"Ever since I learned Kyleigh's birth date, I haven't been able to ignore some of the similarities she and I share. Our riding mannerisms, we're both left-handed, we think algebra is easy." She let out a nervous laugh before sobering. "And her eyes—"

"Stop!" Unable to listen to any more, he shot out of his seat, dragging his fingers through his hair. Barbie's worst fear had been that Ky's birth mother would change her mind and want her baby back, but he'd always discounted her, saying it could never happen.

Pausing at the sink, he gripped the edge as he stared out the window. He'd already lost his wife. He couldn't bear to lose his daughter, too.

"A simple mouth swab is all that's needed for a DNA test."

Was she serious? He whirled to face her. "There will be *no* DNA test." He clenched and unclenched his hands as heat burned in his core. How had she found out? "You gave your child away because she wasn't convenient."

"That's not true. It was because—"

"Kyleigh is *my* daughter, you hear me? Mine and Barbie's." His anger ratcheted up as he recalled how Gloriana had slowly wormed her way into their lives. Into his heart. Insisting she could save the rodeo, helping Ky with her training.

He slowly faced her. "You knew all along, didn't you?"

"What?" Her face contorted. "No, I—"

"That's the real reason you came back, isn't it?"

She vehemently shook her head. "No."

"I don't believe you. What, did you use your connections, hire some private investigator to find your long-lost child? Closed adoptions are just that—closed. How did you find out where she was?"

"It was pure speculation." Tears welled, spilling onto her cheeks. "Too many coincidences."

Unfazed, he said, "I don't believe you. Nothing you've ever told me has been the truth. You've been playing me this whole time, just hoping to get your hands on my daughter, haven't you?"

She balled her fists at her sides. "That's a lie!"

He took a deep breath, willing a calm he definitely did not feel. "No, I don't believe it is." He dared a step closer. "I don't want you anywhere near me or my daughter."

Clamping a hand over her mouth, she whirled and ran toward the door, throwing it open before disappearing outside. A moment later, he heard an engine start and the sound of gravel grinding beneath tires as she peeled away.

His body still quivering with fury, he stomped across the room and slammed the door. He must be a fool among fools, believing Gloriana would ever be interested in him.

Returning to the kitchen, he scooped up the paper plate holding his lunch and tossed it into the trash. He wasn't hungry anymore.

Why, God? Just when things were looking up. When I finally had hope again. Why did You let me fall for Gloriana's lies?

Chapter Thirteen

Tears still streaming down her face, Gloriana parked in Mom's garage and then hurried into the mudroom, tossing her purse on the bench before continuing into the kitchen.

"Mom!" she sobbed, coming up short when she realized Bill was there, too. The two of them sat at the table, eating lunch. "Never mind." Suddenly eager to escape, she started toward the family room until her mother grabbed hold of her arm.

"Glory?" Mom stepped in front of her, her brow pinched with worry. "What is it, baby? What's got you so upset?"

"He hates me."

"Who hates you?"

"Justin. He thinks I want to—" Then she remembered her mother didn't know about the baby.

Clearing his throat, Bill came alongside her mother. "I'll leave the two of you to talk." He glanced Gloriana's way. "If there's anything I can do, just holler."

As the front door clicked shut, Mom escorted Gloriana to the couch and sat down beside her.

"I've never seen you so upset. Talk to me, Gloriana."

What if her mother responded the same way Justin had? What if she thought Gloriana had known all along and that was why she came home?

She's going to find out anyway. May as well be from you.

She took a deep breath. "I know you're going to be hurt, and I wish I'd done things differently, but I did what I thought was best at the time."

"Which time?" Confusion weighed heavy in Mom's gaze. "What are you talking about, dear?"

"I was pregnant when Cody left me. That's why he left."

"Pregnant? I don't understand."

"I'm getting there, Mom. Just give me a minute, please."

She patted Gloriana's hand. "Take all the time you need."

Slowly, and with many tears, Gloriana revealed how her life played out in the months following her divorce, culminating with the birth of a baby girl.

"Oh, Glory." Still clutching Gloriana's hands, Mom cried with her. "We would've helped you."

"I know you would have, but I was too ashamed. I felt so foolish for marrying Cody. For not realizing that he was even more self-absorbed than I was. Nothing like getting a taste of your own medicine, huh?"

Mom stroked Gloriana's cheek.

"It was a turning point in my life. One that forced me to grow up."

"What does this have to do with Justin, though? I can't imagine him hating you for giving your baby to someone who wanted a child."

"It's just a suspicion, but…I think Kyleigh might be that child."

Her mother gasped. "What makes you think that?"

Staring into her mother's eyes, she said, "For starters, her eyes are so much like yours. Then I learned she was born the same day as my baby."

"And she was adopted." Mom slumped against the back of the sofa.

"When I suggested a DNA test, Justin lost it." Tears welled once again as she recalled how enraged he'd been. "He thinks that's why I came home. That I'd been searching for her." She met her mother's watery gaze. "Yeah, there were times I wondered about her over the years, what she might look like, but I was always confident that I'd done the right thing and that she was happy with two parents who loved her."

Mom straightened and took hold of Gloriana's hand again. "And she was. Even after her mother passed, God saw to it Kyleigh was surrounded by people who loved—" Her mother's eyes went wide. "Your baby was born June third?"

"Yes."

Her expression softened. "That's why you didn't come home for your daddy's funeral."

Gloriana nodded. "I was too ashamed."

"And all these years I thought you were just being obstinate and selfish." Her mother hugged her. "I'm so sorry, honey."

They both fell silent as Gloriana savored the embrace, soaking her mother's shoulder with her tears.

Finally, Mom pulled away. "Did Justin ever mention anything to you about where they got Kyleigh? What town or hospital?"

Gloriana tried to recall, but she was so focused on how hateful he'd been that she could think of little else.

She shook her head. "No, he didn't. I mentioned I was attending Tech." As much as it pained her, she forced herself to sort through their conversation. "From the moment I mentioned a DNA test, he went into a rant that began with his insistence that I gave my child away because she wasn't convenient and ended with him calling me a liar."

"I'm sure that pained your already aching heart even more."

"Yeah, it did." He hadn't even resembled the man who, just last night, had tenderly kissed her and practically stumbled over himself trying to convince her to stay here at the ranch.

Mom stared curiously at her. "I find it rather strange that he didn't want more information, though. From what you've said, he was simply reacting to your supposition. I would think he'd want some hard evidence."

"I don't know what to think anymore, Mom." But Gloriana should have known better than to trust Justin. He was no different than Cody, saying he cared until she told him something he didn't want to hear. How foolish could she be?

"Unless..." Her mother's brow pinched in thought. "Maybe he put two and two together when you said you were at Texas Tech. If they went to Lubbock to get their baby..." Mom's eyes were wide now.

"I hadn't thought of that. Though it still doesn't explain why he responded so hatefully. I mean, just last night he was doing everything he could to convince me to stay here after the rodeo." She looked at her hands. "He even kissed me."

"Glory." Her mother's voice was very matter-of-fact. "You grew up out here in the country. You know that sometimes even the sweetest animals can turn vicious when they feel threatened. I think Justin was afraid of losing his daughter."

"It isn't my intention to take her away from him. Yet he comes up with some crazy story and acts like I've been plotting to come in and steal Kyleigh." She shook her head.

"Give him some time to calm down and think things through."

"It won't matter. He'll never trust me again. And I don't want to be with someone who always thinks the worst of me." Even if she'd fallen in love with him. She drew in a shuddering breath. "Marlena called while I was at Tori's. The station in Houston wants to interview me."

"When?"

"Early next week. I'm supposed to call her back to confirm."

Sadness shone in her mother's eyes. "Gloriana, I know we've had our share of trouble throughout the years, and we haven't always seen eye to eye. But having you here, getting to know the woman you've become, a godly woman—" Mom grew teary-eyed again "—has been so special. I hate to see you go." Her bottom lip pooched out.

"That makes two of us. But right now, I don't see how I can stay."

"Then at least pray on it before making your decision."

You prayed your way through that conversation with Justin and look how that turned out.

Trusting God is believing He knows what's best even when it doesn't make sense, her pastor back in Nashville always said.

She would choose to trust. "I couldn't do it any other way." Even if it meant walking away from the place she'd finally come to call home.

* * *

He could not, *would not* lose his daughter.

Justin continued to pace between the kitchen and living room, rubbing the back of his neck. *God, haven't I lost enough already?*

He should have known things were too good to be true. That Gloriana would never be interested in a cowboy like him. Yet he'd pursued her, foolishly thinking they stood a chance. As if he could ever make her happy.

Obviously the joke was on him.

A knock pulled him from his thoughts. It'd better not be Gloriana.

Turning on his heel, he strode to the door and jerked it open to find Bill standing on the porch.

"What do you want?"

The man scowled. "Well, Gloriana came into Francie's, cryin' her eyes out, claiming you hated her. And you don't look much better'n she did." The older rancher moved past him to come inside, even though he hadn't been invited. Turning, he gave Justin a once-over. "Don't s'pose you'd care to tell me what's got the two of you wound up tighter'n a two-dollar watch."

Throwing the door closed, Justin said, "Not particularly, but you're probably gonna pester me till I do."

Bill nudged his cowboy hat back a notch. "Son, I don't pester. Though I do have the patience to wait you out."

"Well, I'll give you one thing." Justin moved into the living room. "Everything you said about Gloriana still holds true. That woman cannot be trusted."

Deep lines carved into Bill's brow. "That doesn't sound like the fella who's been spendin' every second he could with her lately."

"Yeah, well, that was before I found out she's been playing me."

"Playing? Son, I've seen the way she looks at you."

He glared at the man. "It was all an act."

"How do you figure that?"

He was so angry, so focused on Gloriana's claim that Ky was her baby, that he couldn't recall many details. "The short version is that Gloriana had a baby and put it up for adoption. Ky is that baby. Now Gloriana thinks she can get her back."

Bill's brows lifted. "She said that?"

"Maybe not exactly, but close enough for me." Justin dragged a hand through his hair and began pacing in front of the fireplace. "Despite all her talk about taking care of her mother, I'm pretty sure Ky is the real reason Gloriana came back here. How she found out where Ky was, though, I'll never know. It was a closed adoption, so we never had any contact with the birth mother." He was rambling, but he didn't care.

Bill watched him move back and forth. "Justin, take it from another cowboy who's prone to flying off the handle. The first thing you need to do is settle down."

He twisted to face the man. "How can I do that when Gloriana wants to steal my daughter?"

"That's the second time you've said as much." Bill's hands went to his hips. "Did Gloriana say that was her intention? To reclaim her long-lost daughter?"

Stopping, Justin mirrored Bill's stance. "She wants a DNA test. What else could that possibly mean?" Suddenly weary, he crossed to the couch and sat, dropping his head in his hands. "I can't lose my daughter, Bill. She's the only thing that kept me going after Barbie died. Without her..." He dragged his hands down his face and stared blankly at the fireplace. "Barbie was a good mother. She'd always wanted a whole passel of kids, and she poured herself into Ky, never complaining. Whenever I'd point out the struggles, she'd tell me she counted it all joy." His lip curled. "Meanwhile, Gloriana gave Ky away because a baby didn't fit into her life."

Bill eased into the recliner. "Did Gloriana tell you that?"

"I didn't give her the opportunity. But given what I've heard about the old Gloriana…" He pressed his palms against his eyes as tears began to fall. "It's not fair, Bill. Why did God take Barbie away? She was the sweetest person you could ever meet. All she ever wanted was to be a good wife and mother. It doesn't make sense that she's gone and—"

"And you're still here?"

Still covering his face, Justin nodded.

"Now we might be gettin' somewhere," said Bill.

The cushion next to Justin gave way, and he felt a strong arm come around his shoulders.

"I know the pain of losing your first love, the one you planned to grow old with. And I also know the guilt we can impose on ourselves when we find we're having similar feelings for another woman."

Justin swiped the backs of his hands over his eyes. "Who said anything about feeling guilty?"

"I did. Weren't you listening?" The corners of Bill's mouth twitched before he rested his elbows on his thighs and clasped his hands. "Now, instead of giving me the condensed version of your conversation with Gloriana, why don't you tell me the whole thing? Otherwise I'll have to head back up the drive and get Gloriana's version."

"You'd take her word over mine?"

"No, I'd listen and winnow out the truth. Just like I'm doing now."

Justin stared at the man who'd once had some pretty harsh words about Gloriana himself.

After a moment, Justin reluctantly retraced his conversation with Gloriana, recalling the way she'd struggled to get the words out as opposed to demanding. And even though he'd heard what she was saying, things somehow got distorted on the way to his brain. Yet as he was being forced to look back—

"While she was looking to see if the dots connected, I'd already connected them. I mean, how many babies do you suppose were born in Lubbock on that day that were adopted?"

"Lubbock is a big city." Bill paused. "And the part about her coming back here because of Kyleigh?"

Justin could only shake his head. "That was probably a stretch. I felt threatened, so I went on the attack." He could still see the look on her face. As though he'd physically struck her. Then he thought about the way she'd looked after he'd kissed her. The light in her eyes that said she trusted him. And his heart sank.

"I messed up, Bill. Gloriana trusted me with the truth, and I turned on her like a rabid animal." He thrust his fingers into his hair. "How could I be so stupid?"

"It's a gift we menfolk are prone to, especially where the opposite sex is concerned."

"Yesterday I was falling in love with Gloriana. Today I was purposely trying to hurt her." Again, he dropped his head in his hands.

"I know I had my doubts, but the Gloriana I've witnessed and gotten to know since she's been home isn't the selfish girl I remember or the conniving one you described when I first got here."

Justin lifted his head to look at the man he'd come to respect.

"On the contrary, she's a caring woman who's aware of her mistakes and is doing everything she can to correct them. Which makes me wonder what harm there'd be if she was Kyleigh's mother. I mean, at her age, she could probably use a little more female influence in her life."

Though the tiny sliver of Justin that was struggling to hold on to his anger wanted to argue, his common sense told him everything Bill had said was the truth. Justin had seen the vulnerable side of Gloriana, something he suspected few people had ever witnessed.

"I need to apologize to Gloriana. That is, if she'll let me. But first I need to talk to Ky."

"Some prayer might be a good idea, too," said Bill.

"Yeah, I owe the big guy an apology, too. Because before you got here, I was blaming Him."

Bill pushed to his feet. "You know, the Bible tells us all things work together for good."

Justin followed suit as the older rancher started for the door.

Resting his hand on the knob, Bill looked back at him. "Wouldn't it be just like God to have you working at the ranch owned by the family of Kyleigh's birth mother?"

Chapter Fourteen

After Bill left, Justin spent the rest of the afternoon praying, berating himself for treating Gloriana so badly and then praying some more. Not to mention practicing the speech he'd soon be presenting to Ky. The one where he'd not only tell her Gloriana was likely her birth mother but where he'd confess he'd behaved despicably and sent the woman away in tears. He'd rather Ky hear it from him first, before she heard the sorry tale from someone else.

Now as he waited in line at the school to pick up his daughter, he couldn't stop thinking about Gloriana, ashamed of how quick he was to condemn her. Where had all those unfounded thoughts come from, anyway? The notion that she'd hired someone to find Ky.

Desperation. The fear of losing Ky had turned him into somebody he didn't even recognize. Barbie would be so disappointed in him, perhaps even more than he was.

Staring out the window as kids began to file out of the school, he thought back on his conversation with Bill, his chest tightening. What must Francie think of her ranch manager? While she was a loving, gracious woman, everyone had their limits. His treatment of Gloriana could easily cost him his job. And he wouldn't blame her in the least.

He startled when the door suddenly opened.

"Hi, Dad." Ky dropped her backpack on the floorboard and hopped into the passenger seat. "So what are we doing for dinner tonight?" She reached for her seat belt. "Are we going to Francie's or is Ms. Gloriana coming to our house? If she's coming to our house—" she fastened the belt and looked at him "—I was thinking…" Her words trailed off, and her smile faded as she met his gaze. "You look terrible."

"I'm feeling pretty rough. We need to talk."

"Did I do something?"

He shook his head. "No. But you're looking at the biggest screwup in the history of screwups."

"Okay, now you sound like me. And it never turns out to be as bad as I think it's going to be."

If only.

As her dark gaze bored into him, he recalled Gloriana mentioning his daughter's eyes before he'd abruptly cut her off. Ky's were darker than Gloriana's hazel ones, and the shape was different. But suddenly there was a familiarity about them.

He swallowed hard. Francie. Only then did it strike him that not only was Francie Gloriana's mother, if what they suspected was true, she was Ky's grandmother.

"I hope you're right, baby girl."

He stopped by Plowman's so Ky could grab a snack before they headed on to the house.

"Let's sit on the couch." He twisted the cap off his Dr Pepper, suddenly remembering he'd never eaten lunch.

"You're so serious, Dad. You're creeping me out."

"Sorry, that wasn't my intention." He eased onto the

right-hand cushion, and she plopped down beside him. "I have something I'd like to ask you, though."

Unwrapping her Twinkie, she watched him.

"Do you ever wonder about your birth mother?"

Her shoulders slumped ever so slightly. "Would you be mad at me if I said I do sometimes? But only since Mom died."

"How could I be mad? Without your birth mother, you wouldn't be here."

Licking her fingers, she gave him a half smile. "I don't dwell on her or anything. But sometimes I wish I had someone—a woman—to talk to about—" she shrugged "—things. Girl stuff. But then I remember that I've got Mrs. Francie and now Ms. Gloriana. I can always talk to them."

"I'm glad they're a part of your life." Francie had taken Ky under her wing from the day they arrived.

"Why did you ask me that?" Eyeing him suspiciously, she took a bite of her snack while he sucked in a breath.

Here goes nothing.

"I learned today that Gloriana had a baby that she gave up for adoption. A baby girl, born in Lubbock, which is where you were born, on the very same day as you." He watched the myriad of emotions play across his daughter's beautiful face, recognizing a resemblance to Gloriana. The shape of her nose and mouth.

"Why didn't she keep the baby?"

"She was young, and her husband left her when he found out she was pregnant." His heart pinched at the thought of how incredibly painful that must've been for her. To have someone you love and trust just turn their back on you. Kind of like he'd done earlier. Not that Gloriana loved him.

His daughter frowned. "He doesn't sound like a very good husband."

"No, he doesn't."

"So how do we find out for sure if I'm that baby?"

Reaching for his Dr Pepper, he said, "The only way we'd know for sure is to do a DNA test."

She winced as he took a swig. "Are they gonna stick me with a needle?"

He shook his head and lowered the bottle. "No, it's as simple as swabbing your mouth."

"Really?"

"Promise."

Lifting a shoulder, she said, "I think it would be really cool if Ms. Gloriana was my mother. I really like her. But I'm afraid to get my hopes up."

He brushed the hair away from Ky's face. "Even if she's not your mother, she's still your friend."

A smile lit up her face as she straightened. "Can we go talk to her?"

"That's…probably not a good idea right now."

"Why not?" Confusion replaced her smile.

"When she shared her suspicions with me earlier this afternoon, I wasn't very nice. Matter of fact, I got pretty angry with her."

Her dark eyes narrowed. "Why?"

"Because I was afraid of losing you."

"Dad…"

Reaching for her hands, he said, "Ky, I owe you an apology."

"For what?"

"For being a hypocrite."

She looked confused.

"All this time I've been hammering the importance of

church and a relationship with God into your head, I've simply been going through the motions."

"What do you mean?"

"I not only blamed myself for your mother's death, I blamed God, too. I was so angry with Him for taking her away from us."

"So why didn't you just tell Him? He's big enough to take it, Dad."

He squeezed tighter. "How'd you get so smart?"

"I pay attention in church."

"Well, I can guarantee I'm going to be paying closer attention from now on. I'm sorry I've been so wrapped up in my own stuff that I haven't given you a hundred percent."

"What are you talking about? You've always been there for me."

"In that case, I'm glad you didn't notice." But he sure had.

"So what about Ms. Gloriana?" She freed her hands and reached for her sponge cake.

"I owe her an apology, too."

"You like her, don't you?" She took a bite. "And I don't mean as a fwiend."

"Don't talk with your mouth full. And yes. But I'm pretty sure I messed that up."

Swallowing, she said, "Just be honest with her, Dad. Tell her you were afraid. She'll understand."

Thoughts of the pain in Gloriana's eyes played across his mind. "I'm not so sure about that."

"I am."

"Aren't you the confident one."

"Because I can tell she likes you, too. And if she's

hurting…" She hesitated a moment. "Dad, Mom would want you to fall in love again."

"How do you know that?"

"All those movies we used to watch. Her favorites were the ones with people who'd lost their husband or wife. She'd always cry, saying, 'Second-chance stories are my favorite.' She called it beauty for ashes."

"She said that?"

"Yep. Even told me that if anything ever happened to her, she wanted me to make sure you didn't 'shut down and vow never to love again.'" She made air quotes with her fingers and rolled her eyes.

"That sounds just like her." He tugged her close and wrapped his arms around her. "Have I told you how much I love you?"

She squeezed him back. "I love you, too, Daddy."

"I promise I will try to make things right with Gloriana. But there's only so much I can do. She trusted me, and I hurt her. She may never trust me again."

His daughter pulled away and looked him in the eye. "Then you're just going to have to keep trying."

After making certain the chickens—the rooster, in particular—were in their coop, Gloriana stepped outside late Friday afternoon, tired of being holed up and feeling more than a little sorry for herself. What she wouldn't give to go for a ride on Shadow, feel the wind in her face. But she didn't want to risk running into Justin. Even if he had calmed down, as her mother supposed, things would be awkward to say the least. Gloriana would rather avoid him altogether.

She'd contacted her agent first thing this morning, giving her the go-ahead on the interview in Houston.

Then was surprised when Marlena called back within an hour to let her know she was on for Monday morning. So, Gloriana spent the rest of the day updating her portfolio, choosing an outfit and trying to get her head back in the game. It had been six weeks since she'd walked out of the station in Nashville, and other than the telephone and internet interviews she'd done for the rodeo, she hadn't even thought about her work.

Wandering into the yard, she reveled in the sun's warmth, wishing she could erase yesterday from her memory. She'd thought being honest with Justin was the right thing to do. She didn't want that or any other secrets between them. Now, she wished she'd kept it to herself. No, she wished she'd never opened her heart to Justin in the first place. Because in doing so, she'd opened herself to heartache. Been there, done that. And she'd promised herself she'd never do it again.

The sounds of hoof beats captured her attention.

Turning, she set a hand over her eyes to block the sun and peered toward the arena to see Kyleigh practicing. Her determination reminded Gloriana of—

Nope, she wasn't going to go there.

She visually followed Kyleigh as she rounded each barrel before racing across the finish line. Only then did she see Justin standing beside the rail, no doubt clocking his daughter's time.

He turned and started toward Kyleigh. Then he glanced in Gloriana's direction and stopped for a moment before continuing on to his daughter.

Gloriana prayed he hadn't seen her. Even so, she wouldn't allow him to chase her into the house. Though she wasn't opposed to hiding, but only so she wouldn't have to look at him.

Moving to the oak tree, she eased into the double swing that hung from a massive branch overhead. Moments later, she heard the crunch of gravel beneath tires and the engine of a UTV growing closer by the second. *God, please let him keep going.*

Instead, the vehicle and the engine came to a stop.

She stayed where she was, staring out over the pasture, her chest squeezing as his footfalls grew closer. Then the gate creaked open. Out of the corner of her eye, she saw him stop a few feet away. *Do not look at him. Do not—*

Like a fool, she turned. Even with the dark circles under his eyes, he was still handsome.

Arms at his sides, he continued to stare at her. "I need to talk to you."

She cleared her throat. "There's really nothing I need to say."

"Then if you'll just listen? And I promise I'll be nice."

She wanted to say no. Wanted to lash into him the way he had done to her. But then she'd end up feeling guilty and having to pray for forgiveness. *God, I'm afraid.*

Reluctantly, she said, "Go ahead."

He hesitated, rubbing his palms against his jeans. "That first day you arrived at Prescott Farms, you called me out, saying that I'd already formed an opinion of you based on things I'd heard, and you were right. I had. Yet time and again, you proved that you didn't fit into that mold. That you'd changed. And I liked what I saw, though I didn't realize just how much until you were bit by that snake. The thought of losing you was almost impossible to bear. That's when I realized I was falling in love with you."

"Love?" Gloriana glared at him. "That was not love I saw when I told you my suspicions about Kyleigh."

He shook his head. "I was afraid of losing my daughter."

"It was never my intent to take Kyleigh away from you. The only reason I told you was because I didn't feel right keeping secrets from you. Relationships are supposed to be built on trust."

"And I jumped to conclusions when I should have heard you out." He sighed. "I'm sorry I hurt you, Gloriana."

Both fell silent for a moment, leaving Gloriana to wonder how things had fallen apart so quickly. If Justin had truly loved her, he wouldn't have reacted so hatefully.

"I may not have listened very well yesterday," he said. "However, I haven't been able to stop thinking about what you said. And I told Ky."

Gloriana looked at him, wondering what he'd told her.

"We think a DNA test would be appropriate."

Her brain must be muddled. "Why?"

"Because Ky was born in Lubbock. At University Medical Center."

Gloriana gasped. Then softly said, "That's where I delivered."

Sounds to her right had her turning to see Kyleigh coming up the drive atop her horse.

"Hi." The girl waved tentatively, and Gloriana's heart skipped a beat.

She motioned for Kyleigh to join them.

Kyleigh dismounted, dropping Pretty Lady's reins before continuing toward them. "I just wanted to say, even if you're not my mom—I mean, biological mom—I hope we can still be friends."

Swallowing around the lump in her throat, Gloriana smiled. "I'd like that very much." Standing, she approached Justin's daughter and hugged her. As the girl's arms wound around her waist, Gloriana savored the embrace, overcome by the thought that, for the first time in almost fifteen years, she might very well be holding her baby girl.

She sniffed and set Kyleigh away from her. "Perhaps we could make some cookies tomorrow. If that's all right with your father."

"I'd like that." She looked at her father.

"So long as you promise to bring some home." Though he was behind Gloriana, she could hear the smile in his voice. Whether Kyleigh realized it or not, she was blessed to have such a special bond with her father. "Are you up for another run?" he continued.

"Sure."

"All right. You go on and I'll be there shortly."

After another quick hug, Kyleigh was on her way. When she'd moved out of earshot, Justin came alongside Gloriana. "I've already checked into the testing. We can get it done in Brenham. Results take about forty-eight hours."

Turning, she looked up at him. "Then what?"

"If it's a match, Ky has a mother again. If it's not, she's still got a really good friend and someone she can count on." He stepped in front of her then. "Whichever way it goes, I'm still going to pursue you. Gloriana, you gave me hope when I'd given up. Hope that I could share my life with someone again, instead of merely existing. And I'm not about to go back now, because some things are worth fighting for. You're worth fighting for."

If only he'd spoken those words to her yesterday. But she couldn't forget. And forgiveness was questionable, no matter how much her wounded heart urged her to believe what he was saying.

Stiffening her spine, she dared to meet his gaze. "I have an interview in Houston Monday morning."

His eyes narrowed slightly, and his jaw clenched, though he never looked away. "I'm sure you'll blow them away. You're a beautiful, talented woman, Gloriana. If returning to television will make you happy, then I pray it'll work out."

Happy? She doubted that. But at least it would keep her busy, leaving her little time to think about what-might-have-beens and the dream that had evaded her once again.

Chapter Fifteen

◦~∙

Baking cookies with Kyleigh on Saturday had been the highlight of Gloriana's weekend. She'd feared things might be awkward or stilted, but with Kyleigh's bubbly personality, Gloriana needn't have worried. It was as though nothing had changed between them, and, for that, she was grateful.

Sunday, she'd gone to church and prepped for her interview. Though thoughts of Justin kept popping into her head, distracting her. Except for church, she hadn't seen him. With his claim that he was still going to pursue her, she'd halfway expected him to come around. Apparently the news about her interview had shut down that notion. Something that should please her. But it didn't.

So when she went to her SUV that Monday morning, dressed in her black pencil skirt, ivory blouse and four-inch black pumps, she was surprised to find a basket on the driver's seat, containing an assortment of bite-size candies, granola bars and nuts, along with two small bottles of water. The attached note card read, *You've got this!*

It took the entire distance to the arched metal Prescott Farms sign to convince herself Justin was simply being nice and she shouldn't read anything into the gesture. Then, as she pulled onto the main road, she cranked up the Christian radio station and sang her heart out until her phone cut in a little over an hour into her drive and Hawkins's name appeared on the dash.

She pressed the button on her steering wheel. "Good morning."

"Are you still en route to your interview?"

"Yes. I'm not too far out, though." As the sun peeked from behind a cloud, illuminating the Houston skyline, she lowered her visor.

"Are you excited?"

"Not like I should be."

"That sounds like a definite no. So what's the problem? Are you nervous?"

"No." Recently she had begun to think God might be moving her in a different direction. One that would keep her in Hope Crossing. Now that door had pretty much slammed shut. "I guess it's because I wasn't planning to go back to work quite so soon. I kind of enjoyed the slower pace of life at the ranch."

"It wouldn't surprise me if you're burned out. Folks see you on TV and think all you do is sit there and interview people, never realizing that when the camera is off you're constantly hustling for stories. You're in a dog-eat-dog profession."

Glancing at the rearview mirror, she released a sigh. "There was a time when I thrived on that."

"Are you saying you've lost your drive?"

"Let's just say I've come to realize there are things far more important than the next scoop."

"Like family?"

"You guessed it."

He cleared his throat. "Mom told me about Kyleigh. And Justin. Personally, I've always liked the guy, but if you want me to put him in his place for coming down on you, I can do it."

Chuckling, she turned on her blinker and checked her blind spot before maneuvering around a slow-moving RV. "I appreciate your willingness to defend my honor, but I don't think that'll be necessary."

"You're a strong woman, Gloriana, always have been. But that had to have been tough, giving up your child."

Her chest tightened along with her grip on the steering wheel. "Hawkins Prescott, I am on my way to a job interview. If you make me cry, I'm going to be on the next flight to Alaska so I can strangle you."

He laughed. "Okay, we'll discuss that later. But I'm still gonna play big brother and give you some advice."

"Yeah, yeah."

"Even if they offer you the job, it's okay to say no."

"So noted." She spotted her exit.

"And before you cast aside what could potentially be something special with Justin, think about extending him a little grace. He's a guy. He's human. But he's got a good heart."

I'm still going to pursue you. Justin's words replayed in her mind as she veered off the highway.

If that was the case, then how come he hadn't come by?

She spotted the television station just ahead. "Are you finished now? I'm about to pull into the parking lot."

"In that case, go get 'em, Sissy. And I'll be praying God leads wherever He wants you to be."

She eased into a parking spot. "Thank you, Bubba." Ending the call, she put the vehicle in Park, turned off the radio and bowed her head. "God, I've never felt as uncertain as I do right now. I've always been so confident. This past week has been filled with some really high highs—" thoughts of Justin's kiss and the way he made her feel special and wanted played across her mind "—and one gut-wrenching low." She refused to pause on that right now. "But I believe You presented this job opportunity for a reason. If it's to take me away from Prescott Farms, then so be it. Better is one day in Your courts than thousands elsewhere."

She drew in a shaky breath. "But if this is not where You've called me, then I pray You will sound the alarms so I will know beyond a shadow of a doubt. In Jesus's name, Amen."

Looking up, she turned off the engine and grabbed her tote. And since she didn't hear so much as a car horn, she got out and made her way into the single-story tan brick building with a two-story glass entry.

Beyond the glass doors, the reception area had a rustic-modern vibe with its wood-look plank floor and black leather lounge chairs grouped around a glass-topped coffee table above a colorful, geometric rug. Gloriana continued toward the curved reception desk near the far wall, noting the illuminated sign above it, proudly displaying the station's call letters and logo.

A woman close to her age looked up as she approached. Smiled. "Good morning. How may I help you?"

"I have an appointment with Renee Garcia."

"Your name, please?"

"Gloriana Prescott."

"Have a seat and I'll let her know you're here." She reached for her phone and paused. "Can I get you anything? Water? Coffee?"

"No, thank you." Gloriana eased into one of the leather chairs, thinking about the basket Justin had left for her. It was thoughtful of him to do that.

I realized I was falling in love with you.

While she'd railed at him when he'd said those words, now they stirred something inside her.

She squeezed her eyes closed. Where were these thoughts coming from? And why now?

"Ms. Prescott?"

Opening her eyes, she saw a lovely dark-haired woman approach. She stood. "Ms. Garcia?"

"Yes, but you can call me Renee." She motioned for Gloriana to follow her. "Let's go to my office."

They continued a short distance down the hallway behind the reception area, dodging a couple of hurried people while the hum of the newsroom vibrated in the air. Until they turned into one of the coziest offices Gloriana had ever seen. Chairs were adorned with decorative pillows and inspirational signs were strategically placed, along with lots of family photos, including one of Renee with a man Gloriana assumed was her husband and three children.

"You have a beautiful family. How long have you been married?"

Renee rounded her desk, smiling. "Ten years." She eased into her chair. "We got off to a rocky start, but with God's help and a lot of prayer—" She clasped her hands atop her wooden desk. "Forgiveness isn't easy, but it's always worth it."

Forgiveness. The word reverberated through Gloriana.

"I've looked over your résumé and watched some of the clips your agent sent over, and I'm quite impressed." Renee went on, talking about the station and the position, but Gloriana didn't hear a thing. She was too focused on that one word. *Forgiveness.*

Ever since she'd returned to Hope Crossing, Gloriana had been seeking redemption for the mistakes of her past. And by the grace of God, many people now saw her differently. And yet here she was, holding tightly to her anger, at her father and at Justin. Not only had he explained why he'd reacted so strongly and apologized to her, but Justin had been man enough to tell his daughter what he'd done. Gloriana was the one who wasn't willing to let it go.

"Gloriana?"

She looked across the desk to find Renee watching her.

"Is everything all right?"

Reaching for her leather tote on the floor beside her chair, Gloriana stood. "You're right, Renee. Forgiveness is the key." She slung the bag over her shoulder. "I'm so sorry to have wasted your time, but this isn't where I'm supposed to be." Everyone she'd ever loved—with the exception of her brother—was at Prescott Farms. Mom, Justin, Kyleigh. Even if Justin's daughter wasn't Gloriana's by birth, she loved her, nonetheless.

"Thank you for your time. I'm sure this is an amazing place to work, but it's time for me to go home for good."

Justin had picked a bad day to start working hay. Sitting alone in the cab of the John Deere as he slowly moved back and forth across the hay meadow left him with way too much time to think about Gloriana and her interview. Now he wished he'd done something over the weekend, some grand gesture that might have convinced her to stay. In the end, he'd settled on something as lame as leaving a basket of snacks in her car. He could kick himself for not expressing his feelings in the note. Now she probably thought he was eager for her to leave.

Glancing out the window, he eyed the plume of dust trailing the disc mower as he made another pass over the thick green grass. Even if he'd told Gloriana he loved her, she probably wouldn't have believed him.

That was not love I saw when I told you my suspicions about Kyleigh.

She was right. How was he supposed to convince her that his feelings were real after reacting like that?

Time. The one thing he had so little of. The rodeo was just a little over a month away. Though if she got that job in Houston, she might be gone before then.

Staring out the front window, he sucked in a breath. *Lord, I'm at a loss here. I don't know what to do or say for fear I'll make matters even worse. Only You know my heart. You're the one Who changed my heart and allowed me to love again. Where do I go from here?*

He'd just started another row when a vehicle pulled alongside the gate. And his heart skidded to a stop when he realized it was Gloriana's. What was she doing here?

She got out, looking as though she'd come straight from her interview, and leaned her hip against the front bumper, arms crossed, her sunglasses-covered eyes aimed in his direction.

He continued to the end of the row before turning off the tractor, climbing down and walking some fifty feet to where she stood. With the afternoon sun bearing down on him, he tried to gauge her mood, but her expression gave away nothing.

Stopping in front of her, he said, "Problem?"

"A pretty big one." The tone of her voice was very matter-of-fact, and his gut tightened when she moved her sunglasses to the top of her head and those pretty eyes bored into him. "There's something I forgot to tell you."

"What's that?"

Her expression softened. "I forgive you."

He must've looked like a fool, standing there, blinking, trying not to read too much into what she was saying.

"And there's something else." She stepped forward until she was close enough for him to smell the sweet scent of honeysuckle. Then she looked up at him. "I love you."

His heart thumped like crazy as he continued to stare down at her, wondering if he was dreaming. If so, he didn't ever want to wake up. Still, he had to ask.

"What about the job in Houston?"

The warm breeze tossed her hair about.

Reaching up, she brushed it away from her face. "That's not where I want to be."

Did he dare ask? Yes, he was curious, but then, curiosity hadn't turned out so well for that cat.

He had to know, though. "Where do you want to be?"

"Home. Here at Prescott Farms. With you."

Moving his hands to her arms, he lowered his forehead to hers. "You have no idea how incredibly happy that makes me." Trailing his fingers down her arms, he took her hands in his. "I love you, too. And I promise to show you just how much each and every day." Lifting his head, he cupped her face and kissed her with an intensity he hoped left no doubt about his feelings for her.

When he finally managed to pull himself away, he smiled. "You taste like chocolate."

"Oh, yeah?" She rested her palms against his chest. "This guy I've been eyeing for a while left some in my car."

"Sounds kinda lame to me."

"Justin, chocolate is never lame." Looking past him to the tractor, she said, "How much longer do you think you'll be?"

Keeping one arm around her waist, he surveyed the pasture. "An hour. Maybe a little more." Facing her again, he hesitated. "I made an appointment for Ky to have a DNA test."

The uncertain look in her eyes nearly undid him. "When?" The word was barely a whisper. She was afraid. And it was his fault.

"This afternoon. After school." He tightened his hold on her. "Actually, I made two appointments. In case you'd like to join us."

Her smile was tremulous. "I'd like that very much."

"In that case, why don't I finish up here and I'll meet you back at Francie's?"

"Okay." She turned to walk away, but he tugged her to him once again.

"Not so fast." He claimed her lips one more time as hope coursed through his veins. God had not only granted him a second chance at love, but He'd offered a second chance with the woman who'd stirred his heart and made him dare to love again. And somehow, with God's help, Gloriana would never doubt his love ever again.

Thursday evening, Gloriana paced the family room, dressed in a casual floral dress, waiting for Justin and Kyleigh to arrive while Mom put the finishing touches on dinner with Bill at her side. Justin and Gloriana had picked up the test results this morning but decided to wait until everyone was together so they could all find out at once.

"Glory, stop that pacing," Mom hollered from the

kitchen. "You're making me nervous, and we have nothing to be nervous about."

"I'm sorry." She wrung her hands. "I know that no matter what the results are they're not going to change anything between me and Justin or me and Kyleigh. Still, what if they do?"

Her mother laughed. "Are you even listening to yourself?"

The doorbell rang, and Gloriana hurried to get it. And when she flung the door open, her heart caught in her throat.

Justin stood there—freshly showered, she guessed, from his damp hair—holding a bouquet of red roses. Beside him, his daughter bounced on the balls of her flip-flops in a cute yellow sundress, her dark hair curled and spilling over her shoulders. She, too, held a bouquet, a colorful mix of pink, purple, yellow and white flowers.

"Hi." The word rushed out on Gloriana's breath as she clung to the door handle.

"You look amazing." Justin's eyes glimmered as he stepped inside and kissed her cheek.

Kyleigh followed, and Gloriana closed the door.

"These are for you." He held out the roses.

"They're beautiful." She took hold of the bouquet and inhaled their sweet fragrance before looking up at him. "Thank you."

"And I got you these." Kyleigh looked as nervous as Gloriana felt as she handed off her flowers.

"I love them. The mix of colors is so fun and happy." She laid them atop the other bouquet, allowing her to wrap her free arm around Kyleigh's shoulders. "Thank you, sweetie." Releasing the girl, she looked from Kyleigh to her father. "You two make me feel so special."

Justin smiled. "We happen to think you are *extra* special." The way he looked at her erased any doubts she might have had.

"Y'all come on in here." Mom motioned them into the family room. "Dinner is ready whenever we are, but I know we have something important to tackle first." Her gaze moved from Gloriana to Justin to Kyleigh. "That is, unless you'd prefer to eat first."

"No," the trio said in unison.

"Let me just put these in some water." Gloriana started toward the kitchen.

"Bill," her mother hollered behind her, "grab a pitcher from the cupboard and put some water in it. Glory, the flowers will be fine in there until we can get to them."

Gloriana was beginning to think her mother was just as eager to find out the test results as she was.

Nerves settled over her once again when she returned to the family room. For a week now her mind had been bouncing back and forth over the possibility of Kyleigh being her daughter. A part of her—okay, a big part—selfishly hoped she was. But regardless of whether she was or wasn't, it wouldn't change how Gloriana felt about this precious girl. She loved Kyleigh.

Justin retrieved the manila envelope that had been sitting ominously on the kitchen counter all afternoon. "Is everyone ready?"

They all nodded.

He undid the clasp before pulling out the results. He studied them for what seemed like forever before he smiled and handed them to Gloriana.

Her hand shook as she took hold of the paper. She scanned the page, the litany of numbers meaning very little. Her search came to a halt on the words *Probabil-*

ity of Maternity. To the right of that were numbers that left no room for doubt. She was Kyleigh's birth mother.

Suddenly unsteady, she eased onto the sofa, pressing a hand to her mouth as she continued to stare at the paper.

"What does it say?" Kyleigh asked.

A lump formed in Gloriana's throat when Justin said, "It says she's your mother."

Mom let go a tearful gasp.

But Gloriana couldn't seem to stop staring at the results for fear they might change if she looked away.

Then Kyleigh moved beside her. "Ms. Gloriana?" She sat down. "Are you okay?"

Nodding, Gloriana set the paper aside and took hold of the girl's hands. Her daughter's hands. Through a veil of tears, she stared into Kyleigh's eyes.

"I have loved you your whole life. And the one and only time I held you in my arms and looked into your eyes, I did something I didn't normally do back then. I prayed and asked God to watch over you. Now He's allowed me to see for myself that He did just that by giving you two amazing parents. I gave you life, but it's because of your mom and dad that you are the happy, tenderhearted, godly girl you are today."

A tear streaked down Kyleigh's face, and Gloriana reached to wipe it away with her thumb, her palm lingering on her daughter's cheek. "Saying goodbye to you was the hardest thing I've ever done. And I hope you won't fault me for that."

The girl adamantly shook her head.

Then Gloriana hugged her daughter, savoring the gift God had given her. "I love you, Kyleigh."

"I love you, too."

Gloriana could only hold her tighter.

When they finally parted, Gloriana smiled. "Would you like to meet your grandmother?"

Grinning, Kyleigh nodded.

They both stood, and Kyleigh promptly scurried across the room into Francie's waiting embrace.

Gloriana felt Justin's arm come around her waist, and she leaned into him. "I feel so incredibly blessed. Thank you for allowing me to be a part of her life."

Then he touched her chin, urging her to look up at him. "Thank *you* for being a part of ours."

Epilogue

What a week! Seven days ago Gloriana had had the privilege of serving as maid of honor at her mother's wedding, then she got to celebrate her daughter's birthday for the very first time on Wednesday and now, under a starry sky with the aromas of cotton candy, popcorn and barbecue mingling with the sounds of the midway, she would soon watch Luke Phillips take the stage at the dance hall, culminating this year's Hope Crossing Fair and Rodeo.

Standing just outside the historic building, she admired the string lights crisscrossing over the large wooden dance floor positioned nearby and surrounded by bleachers on three sides. Speakers had been strategically placed, and there was even a big screen that would simulcast the concert taking place inside the dance hall so those outside wouldn't miss a thing. She'd worked closely with the rental company to make sure they were able to accommodate as many people as possible, and it did her heart good to see that vision come to life as fairgoers filled the stands.

"This is definitely *not* the Hope Crossing Fair and Rodeo I remember."

Gloriana turned at the sound of Mandy Brinkman's voice to see her smiling as she held the hand of her obviously adoring fiancé, Landon Hightower. "Isn't it great?"

Mandy studied the outdoor setup. "You are absolutely amazing." Her gaze shifted back to Gloriana. "I can't believe you did all of this."

She held up her hands. "Trust me, it was a team effort."

"Maybe so, but you were the captain."

"Thank you both for taking the time to come out here today. For signing all those autographs. I'm sure you're exhausted."

Landon chuckled. "It was a whole lot easier than going eight seconds on a bull." He had a point.

"Not quite as painful, I hope."

"No, ma'am."

Gloriana looked from him to Mandy and back. "We have seats reserved for the two of you inside."

"As if we'll be sitting all that much. I'm ready for some dancin'." Mandy looked inside the building. "I'm totally loving the vibe of this place. It'd be a great wedding venue." She faced Gloriana again. "Which, of course, we happen to be looking for."

Gloriana couldn't help but smile. The board had recently agreed to do some renovations to the place, updating the restrooms and adding a commercial kitchen, for that very purpose. "Hmm, sounds like we'll be talking again soon."

"You can count on it," said Mandy.

As she and her intended made their way into the dance hall, Gloriana spotted Tori coming around the corner, looking super cute in a sundress and cowgirl boots.

"Hey, girlfriend," Tori said with a smile.

"Hey, yourself." Gloriana hugged her. "I was afraid you weren't coming."

"And miss my one and only opportunity to see Luke Phillips? No way. I had to get Aiden settled at his grandmother's, though."

"Well, I'm glad you're here now."

"Where's that daughter of yours?" Tori had been thrilled when Gloriana told her the results of the DNA test.

"Wandering around with her father and grandparents, and my brother." Both Justin's and Barbie's parents had come in to watch their granddaughter's first rodeo. Something Gloriana had been a little nervous about. To her surprise, though, they'd embraced her and made her feel as though she was a part of the family.

She checked her watch. "They were supposed to be here by now. Mom and Bill are already inside." Out of the corner of her eye, Gloriana saw Charlene approaching. Her bright coral sundress and wide smile were hard to miss.

"Yeah, if you need me, I'll be inside with Francie." Obviously, Tori had seen her, too.

"Oh sure, throw me to the wolves."

While Tori disappeared into the dance hall, Charlene stopped beside Gloriana, seemingly breathless. "You aren't going to believe this. Based on ticket sales, this year's fair and rodeo has had the largest turnout in its history."

"Awesome." Gloriana high-fived the woman.

"It gets even better," Charlene continued. "Not only will the Texas Pit Masters group be adding us to their circuit, I've been assured by the Lone Star Junior Rodeo Association that Hope Crossing will continue to be a part of their circuit, as well. With one *little* caveat."

Gloriana couldn't imagine what more they could possibly want. "What's that?"

"That we don't go back to the ho-hum fair and rodeo we've had in recent years."

"I see." If Gloriana had her way, the event would never be thought of as ho-hum again.

Charlene's shoulders rose and fell as she took a deep breath. She sheepishly met Gloriana's gaze. "We couldn't have pulled this off without you, Gloriana. And with all of the ideas you've given us to provide a steadier stream of income... What I'm trying to say is, would you please consider serving on the rodeo board?"

She stared at the woman who'd once been her nemesis. "I—I'm honored you would ask, Charlene. Do you mind if I think about it, though? I'm a little overwhelmed at the moment."

"Aren't we all." She fanned herself with the papers she held in her hand. "You know how to get in touch with me."

Gloriana watched the woman walk away, still in shock. Never in a million years would she have expected Charlene to compliment her, let alone want to work with her. *God, You are amazing.* Gloriana's life had changed so much since returning to Hope Crossing.

She checked her watch again. Where was everyone? They were supposed to meet her here ten minutes ago.

"Excuse me." An unfamiliar man, tall, late fifties, approached. "Are you Gloriana Prescott?"

"Yes, sir."

"My name is Ken Mahan." He extended his hand. "I'm with the Bluebird Chamber of Commerce." Bluebird was in the next county over.

"It's nice to meet you." She shook his hand.

"I've heard that you're responsible for reviving this event."

"Mr. Mahan, I'm sure you know as well as I do that an event like this is a team effort."

"Yes, ma'am. However, sometimes things can grow stagnant until someone comes along and breathes new life into them." Shifting from one cowboy-booted foot to the next, he retrieved his wallet from the back pocket of his jeans. He pulled out a business card. "We have a festival every spring that could use a little boost. If you're available for consultations or could assist us with promotion, I'd like to speak with you."

She stared at the card as the sound of the crowd continued to swell around them. Mr. Mahan wasn't the first person to approach her. She'd already been contemplating starting her own business. Something that would allow her to work with small towns to help promote their events.

Nodding, she said, "I'll be in touch."

As Mr. Mahan continued toward the bleachers, Gloriana felt a hand slip around her waist. Lifting her gaze, she saw Justin smiling down at her, and her heart thundered like Kyleigh's horse racing into the arena. Gracious, he was a handsome man.

"I was wondering where you were."

She stepped back, allowing his family and her brother to join them.

"We were on Luke Phillips's bus!" Kyleigh all but squealed.

"That's exciting," said Gloriana.

"I made Dad take, like, a gazillion pictures of me with him and his band. It was *so* cool! And they all congratulated me on my win." Kyleigh had taken third place in today's competition. Pretty amazing considering it was her first year.

"Where are Bill and Francie?" Justin rested his hand

against the small of her back, making her feel protected.
Wanted.

"They're already inside with Tori."

"We'd better get in there, too." Kyleigh motioned to
her grandparents. "Come on."

Justin took hold of Gloriana's hand and led her into
the building with old wood floors and exposed rafters.
Every shutter in the place stood wide, allowing what
little breeze there was to flow through the windowless
openings while overhead fans aided the effort. Wooden
tables and chairs that had been in the dance hall forever
lined the walls on each side, leaving the rest of the space
open for dancing.

After stopping several times to greet friends, they
joined the rest of the family at a large table near the
stage, where a drum set and several guitars awaited their
players. Strings of lights glowed overhead while country music echoed from speakers, and the entire space
hummed with anticipation.

As they neared their family and friends to the left of
the stage, Hawkins took hold of her elbow. Since Mom's
wedding and the rodeo were the same week, not to mention his niece's birthday, he'd scheduled an extended visit,
and Gloriana had enjoyed every minute she'd been able
to spend with him. Now if she could only talk him into
moving back home.

She leaned closer.

"You done good, Sissy. Clay would be very proud of
everything you did here."

She smiled, thinking of the man who'd taught her to go
after her dreams. Though she never would've imagined
that those dreams would bring her back to Hope Crossing. Now she couldn't imagine leaving.

She'd just slipped into a chair between Justin and Tori

when whoops erupted both inside and outside the dance hall. Looking up, she saw the band making their way onto the stage, and the cheers grew even louder when Luke Phillips appeared.

"How's it going, Hope Crossing?"

The crowd was on their feet now.

"Let me tell ya," he continued, "y'all sure know how to do things up right. Has this been a great day or what?"

The cheers continued.

"Before we get started tonight, I'd like to ask Ms. Gloriana Prescott and Justin Broussard to join me up here on the stage for a special announcement."

Gloriana looked at Justin. "I don't know anything about a special announcement."

He shrugged and took hold of her hand. Perhaps it had to do with turnout numbers.

After they'd climbed the trio of steps that led to the stage, Justin urged her take the lead. Pausing next to Luke, she eyed the singer curiously. "What's up?"

After a couple of whoops, the crowd fell silent as he smiled and motioned for her to turn around. When she did, she saw Justin on one knee, holding a tiny box in his hand that bore a sparkling diamond ring.

Her heart all but stopped beating.

His smile kind of wobbled as he peered up at her. "Gloriana Prescott, I love you with all of my heart. Will you marry me?"

Her smile was instantaneous. Without hesitating, she said, "Yes!"

As applause erupted once again, he stood and slid the ring on her finger as Kyleigh appeared at the edge of the stage.

"Dad, you didn't tell me you were going to do that."

He pulled Gloriana close, his smile filled with the

same joy overflowing from her heart. "Didn't need to. I figured you'd approve." Then he lowered his head and kissed Gloriana with an intensity that left her breathless.

A round of hugs ensued when they rejoined their family and friends, including a ferocious one from Kyleigh.

"Does this mean I can call you Mom?" Gloriana had insisted her daughter drop the Ms. from her name after they learned she was her mother.

"I'd love nothing more, but we can discuss that later with your dad."

As the band began to play, Gloriana found herself basking in the wonder of God's many blessings. She'd come back to Hope Crossing to care for her mother and, hopefully, make up for the many mistakes of her past, never dreaming she'd find so much more. By the grace of God, her life had been transformed. Her past had been redeemed, and she'd learned to trust again.

As people flooded the dance floor, Justin reached for her hand. His smile sparkled in his blue-green eyes. "Care to join me?"

They'd come a long way since that day she returned to Prescott Farms. Battled back from preconceived notions, misunderstandings and wounded pasts to find something rare and unexpected. A love she wouldn't trade for the world. And soon, they'd be a family.

Feeling as though her heart might burst, she settled her hand in his. "Always."

* * * * *

If you enjoyed this book in Mindy Obenhaus's Hope Crossing series, look for the next book coming in December 2022 from Love Inspired!

Dear Reader,

Welcome to Hope Crossing, Texas! I hope you enjoyed Justin and Gloriana's story. These two characters had a lot to overcome—not only distrust and preconceived notions, but their pasts and the scars left behind. Forgiveness is rarely easy, but true and earnest forgiveness is healing. Sometimes even more so for the one offering it up than the one receiving it. And yes, I speak from experience.

Through the course of writing this book, I fell in love with its characters. I admire Gloriana's grit and her determination to right her wrongs. I appreciate Justin's fierce loyalty and desire to protect those he loves, even if he sometimes flies off the handle without thinking first. Kyleigh's exuberance and the joy with which she embraces each new experience reminds me of one of my granddaughters. Even Francie and Bill tugged at my heartstrings. And you can be certain you'll be seeing most of them again in upcoming books. Starting with a story about Gloriana's brother, Hawkins.

Until then, I would love to hear from you. You can contact me via my website, mindyobenhaus.com, or find me on Facebook—just search for Mindy Obenhaus, author. And don't forget to sign up for my newsletter so you'll be in the know about book releases and giveaways. Just look for the Subscribe to My Newsletter box on my website.

God bless,
Mindy

AN AMISH PROPOSAL FOR CHRISTMAS
Indiana Amish Market • by Vannetta Chapman

Assistant store manager Rebecca Yoder is determined to see the world and put Shipshewana, Indiana, behind her. The only thing standing in her way is training new hire Gideon Fisher and convincing him the job's a dream. But will he delay her exit or convince her to stay?

HER SURPRISE CHRISTMAS COURTSHIP
Seven Amish Sisters • by Emma Miller

Millie Koffman dreams of becoming a wife and mother someday. But because of her plus size, she doubts it will ever come true—especially not with handsome neighbor Elden Yoder. But when Elden shows interest in her, Millie's convinced it's a ruse. Can she learn to love herself before she loses the man loves?

THE VETERAN'S HOLIDAY HOME
K-9 Companions • by Lee Tobin McClain

After a battlefield incident leaves him injured and unable to serve, veteran Jason Smith resolves to spend his life guiding troubled boys with the help of his mastiff, Titan. Finding the perfect opportunity at the school Bright Tomorrows means working with his late brother's widow, principal Ashley Green...*if* they can let go of the past.

JOURNEY TO FORGIVENESS
Shepherd's Creek • by Danica Favorite

Inheriting failing horse stables from her estranged father forces Josie Shepherd to return home and face her past—including her ex-love. More than anything, Brady King fervently regrets ever hurting Josie. Could saving the stables together finally bring peace to them—and maybe something more?

THE BABY'S CHRISTMAS BLESSING
by Meghann Whistler

Back on Cape Cod after an eleven-year absence, Steve Weston is desperate for a nanny to help care for his newborn nephew. When the lone candidate turns out to be Chloe Richardson, the woman whose heart he shattered when they were teens, he'll have to choose between following his heart or keeping his secrets...

SECOND CHANCE CHRISTMAS
by Betsy St. Amant

Blake Bryant left small-town life behind him with no intention of going back—until he discovers the niece he never knew about is living in a group foster home. But returning to Tulip Mound also involves seeing Charlie Bussey, the woman who rejected him years ago. Can he open his heart enough to let them both in?

Get 4 FREE REWARDS!

We'll send you 2 FREE Books plus 2 FREE Mystery Gifts.

FREE Value Over $20

Both the **Love Inspired**® and **Love Inspired**® **Suspense** series feature compelling novels filled with inspirational romance, faith, forgiveness, and hope.

YES! Please send me 2 FREE novels from the Love Inspired or Love Inspired Suspense series and my 2 FREE gifts (gifts are worth about $10 retail). After receiving them, if I don't wish to receive any more books, I can return the shipping statement marked "cancel." If I don't cancel, I will receive 6 brand-new Love Inspired Larger-Print books or Love Inspired Suspense Larger-Print books every month and be billed just $6.24 each in the U.S. or $6.49 each in Canada. That is a savings of at least 17% off the cover price. It's quite a bargain! Shipping and handling is just 50¢ per book in the U.S. and $1.25 per book in Canada.* I understand that accepting the 2 free books and gifts places me under no obligation to buy anything. I can always return a shipment and cancel at any time by calling the number below. The free books and gifts are mine to keep no matter what I decide.

Choose one: ☐ **Love Inspired**
Larger-Print
(122/322 IDN GRDF)

☐ **Love Inspired Suspense**
Larger-Print
(107/307 IDN GRDF)

Name (please print)

Address   Apt. #

City   State/Province   Zip/Postal Code

Email: Please check this box ☐ if you would like to receive newsletters and promotional emails from Harlequin Enterprises ULC and its affiliates. You can unsubscribe anytime.

Mail to the **Harlequin Reader Service:**
IN U.S.A.: P.O. Box 1341, Buffalo, NY 14240-8531
IN CANADA: P.O. Box 603, Fort Erie, Ontario L2A 5X3

Want to try 2 free books from another series? Call **1-800-873-8635** or visit www.ReaderService.com.

---

*Terms and prices subject to change without notice. Prices do not include sales taxes, which will be charged (if applicable) based on your state or country of residence. Canadian residents will be charged applicable taxes. Offer not valid in Quebec. This offer is limited to one order per household. Books received may not be as shown. Not valid for current subscribers to the Love Inspired or Love Inspired Suspense series. All orders subject to approval. Credit or debit balances in a customer's account(s) may be offset by any other outstanding balance owed by or to the customer. Please allow 4 to 6 weeks for delivery. Offer available while quantities last.

Your Privacy—Your information is being collected by Harlequin Enterprises ULC, operating as Harlequin Reader Service. For a complete summary of the information we collect, how we use this information and to whom it is disclosed, please visit our privacy notice located at corporate.harlequin.com/privacy-notice. From time to time we may also exchange your personal information with reputable third parties. If you wish to opt out of this sharing of your personal information, please visit readerservice.com/consumerschoice or call 1-800-873-8635. **Notice to California Residents**—Under California law, you have specific rights to control and access your data. For more information on these rights and how to exercise them, visit corporate.harlequin.com/california-privacy.

LIRLIS22R2

HARLEQUIN
PLUS

Announcing a **BRAND-NEW** multimedia subscription service for romance fans like you!

Read, Watch and Play.

Experience the easiest way to get the romance content you crave.

Start your **FREE 7 DAY TRIAL** at www.harlequinplus.com/freetrial.